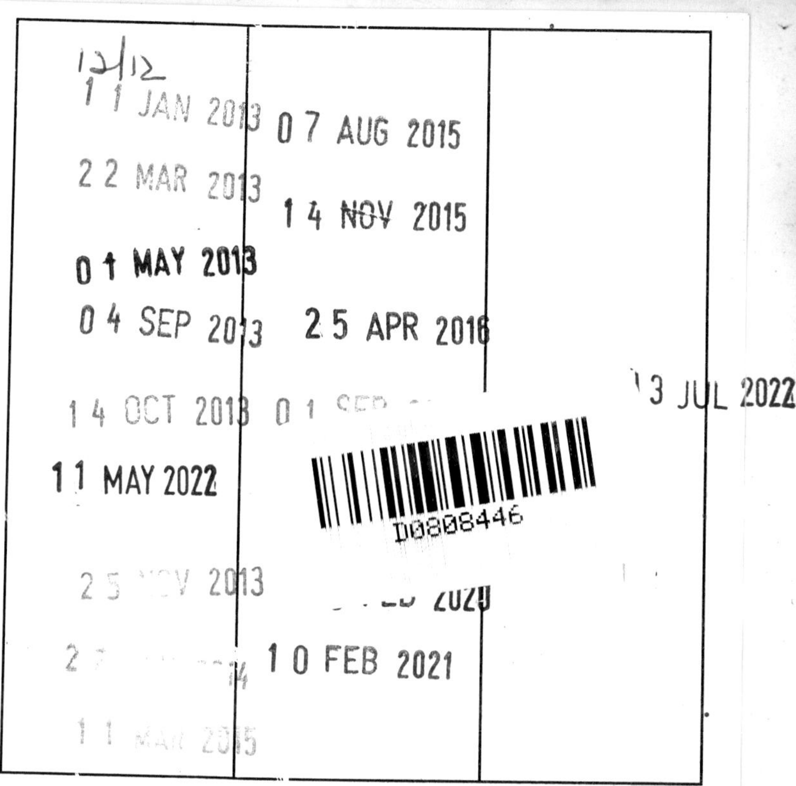

THE BRIGHTER BOROUGH
Wandsworth

nosy
crow

For KJG, for everything

First published in the UK in 2011 by Nosy Crow Ltd
The Crow's Nest, 11 The Chandlery
50 Westminster Bridge Road
London, SE1 7QY, UK

A CIP catalogue record for this book will be available from the British Library

P… Types… re
Pap… sustainable forests

ISBN: 978 0 85763 016 2

www.nosycrow.com

Chapter One

Olivia Marvell stood on the pavement in the pouring London rain. She screwed up her eyes as she lifted her face to the sky and the rain lashed down so hard it was like hundreds of tiny pinpricks. Olivia sighed. Even the weather had a grudge against her. She glanced at her dad, Jack, who since they had left the Tube station had been wrestling with an umbrella that kept being caught by the wind and turning itself inside out. The umbrella was clearly going to win. Jack looked as cold, wet and miserable on the outside as Olivia felt inside. She shivered. She hated London already; she had only been here for a few hours, and longed for the Italian late-summer sunshine that made you want to arch your back and stretch like a cat.

In one hand Olivia held a battered, bulging suitcase out of which poked a sodden, slightly muddy pyjama leg and the end of a thick wire; in the other she was holding the hand of Eel, her little sister. Eel hadn't been christened Eel, of course, but had acquired the nickname soon after birth because she was such a wriggly little thing, never still for a minute. She was jiggling around now, pulling on Olivia's hand, but Olivia only held on tighter.

"Cut it out, Eel! Anyone would think you were seven months old, not seven years," said Olivia irritably.

A few passers-by eyed them curiously, and one smartly dressed woman crossed over the road as if to avoid the raggle-taggle group.

"Bet she thinks that we're going to beg for money or mug her," muttered Olivia fiercely.

"You can't blame her," said Eel sadly, shaking her chestnut curls like a dog and spraying Olivia's face with more water. "We look rubbish. We probably pong too," she said, sniffing herself like a bloodhound. She was wrong about that, but they did look a mess. Olivia's hair was stuck damply to her face while Eel had a big smudge on her forehead and her skirt was torn after an unfortunate encounter with the ticket barriers at the Tube station. Eel had never seen ticket barriers before and had decided she never wanted to see them again. They had appeared determined to gobble her up.

"Come on, girls," said Jack, abandoning his tussle with the umbrella. "We'll be soaked through if we stand here any longer. Let's just walk fast. It's not very far." They set off at a brisk pace, even though it made Jack limp badly, and as they turned the corner of the street, an imposing red-brick building came into view. At the front of the building a sign written in large black letters declared "The Swan Academy of Theatre and Dance". In smaller letters below it said "An academic and performing arts education for talented children aged 7–16". Underneath that was written in italics: *"Proprietor: Alicia Swan"*.

"Here we are," said Jack, coming to a halt opposite the building and dragging them into a shop doorway for shelter.

Olivia's mouth fell open as she read the sign, and then she turned to her father and said accusingly, "It's a *stage* school. You said that we were going to stay with our grandmother and go to her school. You didn't tell us that she runs a *stage school*." Olivia spat out the words "stage school" as if they had a nasty taste.

Jack looked like a small boy who had just been caught with his fingers in the sweet jar. "Didn't I? I must have forgotten to mention it."

Olivia glared at him. "But you've always said that you hate all that fake theatre stuff, and so do we."

"Not me," piped up Eel. "I've always wanted to learn to dance but we've never stayed anywhere long enough to have lessons." She tried to do a little twirl and got tangled up with Olivia, who was still gripping her hand. "I'll be a great dancer. The bestest."

"You can't say bestest," said Olivia witheringly.

"I can if I want," said Eel, but she looked as if she might cry.

"I'm sure you'll be a fantastic dancer," said Jack soothingly, but Olivia detected a note of false cheerfulness in his tone.

"But what about me?" demanded Olivia. "I can't dance and I won't dance, and I don't want to go to stage school either. I want to stay with you and carry on walking the high-wire.

I'm a circus artist, not a stage-school brat."

Jack looked at his elder daughter, at her determined mouth and flashing eyes, and for a moment thought that his beloved wife, Toni, had suddenly come back to life. He shook his head sadly before swallowing hard and declaring a little too heartily, "Well, there is a choice. It's stage school or the orphanage run by a wicked old witch who eats children for breakfast."

"Well, I vote for stage school," said Eel, hopping from one leg to another, "and Livy will have to come too because she's superglued herself to me and is holding my hand so hard it hurts."

"That's because you can't be trusted!" said Olivia, the words exploding out of her mouth like a stuck cork suddenly released from the neck of a bottle. "It's all your fault that we're in this situation. If you hadn't. . ." She tailed off as she saw Eel and Jack's faces, white with shock. Olivia's anger evaporated as quickly as it had materialised and she burst into loud, guilty tears.

"Oh Eel, I didn't mean it! I'm really, really sorry," she sobbed. "I know it was an accident. It's just everything feels so miserable, and I'm tired of pretending everything is all right when it's not."

Eel hugged her and said tearfully, "It's OK, Livy. But we've got to make the best of things." She moved her head close to Olivia's and whispered, "We've got to be as brave as llamas and very cheerful. For Dad's sake, cos he hardly ever smiles now."

"I think you mean lions, Eel. Llamas probably aren't that brave. But you're right, Dad is so sad and defeated all the time." And, as if somebody had turned on a hosepipe, Olivia's tears started flowing again.

"He looks just like my teddy bear looked after he accidentally got put in the washing machine on an extra-hot wash," replied Eel sadly. "If it was an accident," she added ominously.

"It's nobody's fault," said Jack firmly. "We've just had some bad luck, my lovelies, but our luck will change."

"Look," said Eel, sniffing and pointing at the sky, "it's changing already. It's stopped raining and the sun has come out. I might even dry out if Livy would only stop crying all over me." Olivia gave a wan smile and hiccupped.

"So, Liv, what's it to be: the orphanage or

stage school?" asked her father.

Olivia looked at Eel and Jack's expectant faces and felt more ashamed of her outburst than ever. She took a deep breath and whispered, "Stage school."

"That's lucky," said Eel with a grin, "because Dad is too old for an orphanage."

"I'm far too ancient for stage school, too," said Jack with a boyish laugh, but when Olivia caught his eye, he looked away guiltily.

Chapter Two

"What time is Granny Alicia expecting us all?" asked Olivia, licking the icing off a chocolate and raspberry cupcake.

"We'll be going across to the Swan soon, very soon," said Jack, looking at his watch.

"Why does it matter if we're a bit early?" asked Olivia, shrugging her shoulders.

"Your gran's a very busy woman," said Jack evasively. They were sitting in a café across the road from the Swan and opposite a large, boarded-up building that was next door to the stage school. Jack had produced a tattered five-pound note and some loose change from his pocket and suggested that they use the last of their money to go to the café to get warm. They were 10p short for the food and drinks but the café owner was so charmed by Jack, and Eel's cheeky grin, that she even threw in a free espresso. Jack rewarded her with a dazzling smile that made him look young and carefree for a second.

Olivia had taken her little sister to the toilet to smarten up a bit. They still looked extremely shabby, but no longer quite so disreputable. Olivia had even managed to disguise the hole in Eel's skirt with a craftily placed safety pin.

The girls both had lemonade and cupcakes and Jack had positioned himself so he could watch out the window. A succession of cars were pulling up outside the Swan and dropping children off. The door of the café jangled and Olivia watched as a mother and daughter – who she thought looked like two blonde peas in a pod – came in, ordered hot chocolate and tea, and sat down. The girl, with fair hair, rosebud mouth, a tilt-tipped nose and startling blue eyes, was wearing leg warmers and a leotard with a short skirt on top. A pair of worn jazz shoes lay on top of some clothes in an open bag. Eel eyed the shoes with interest and hoped that she'd soon have a pair just like them, only newer and shinier.

Olivia glanced shyly at the girl, who she guessed was probably around twelve, the same age as her. The girl gave her a quick smile. She looked nice, thought Olivia, a bit like a doll she had loved when she was little. The girl was clearly a Swan pupil and Olivia wondered whether they might be in the same class and become friends. The girl's mother kept glancing at her watch so anxiously that she made Olivia think of the White Rabbit in *Alice in Wonderland*.

"I'm terribly sorry, Georgia darling, but I really do have to go soon." The girl's mouth tightened as if she was struggling not to cry. The woman fumbled in her bag and brought out a small box, simply but beautifully wrapped. She pushed it towards her daughter. Eel nudged Olivia, and both of them watched what was going on at the next table while pretending that they were deeply engrossed in nibbling the remaining icing off their cakes.

"This is for you, Georgia." The girl's eyes widened in surprise. Eel craned her neck to get a better look.

"For me? It's not my birthday."

The woman smiled. "I know it's not, but it *is* an important day for you. Your first solo performance. I'm so proud of you and I wanted you to have something to remember it by."

"You shouldn't go round buying me things; you're always telling me we haven't got any money. We don't even have enough for any new jazz shoes."

"I didn't buy it, Georgia," said the woman with a sigh. "Open it," she coaxed.

The girl picked up the little package and carefully unwrapped it. Inside was a small box. She opened it and held a Victorian posy ring aloft, an arrangement of topaz and garnet that sparkled when it caught the light. Olivia thought the ring was beautiful; it reminded her of the ruby and emerald engagement ring that her mum had always worn when she was alive. Jack kept it safe in a box and had told Olivia it would one day belong to her.

"It's Granny's ring, the one she gave to you," said Georgia to her mum, wonderingly.

"Yes, it is. But I want you to have it. To mark today." Olivia was surprised to see Georgia's lips tremble and her eyes well with tears.

"It's beautiful, but I can't take it. It's yours and I know how much it means to you. It's the only thing that you've got to remember her by," she said, pushing the ring back towards her mum. Eel nudged Olivia again, but the entire café was now transfixed by the unfolding drama.

"But it's your special day, your big moment," said her mother. Georgia stood up suddenly, knocking over her chair. Hot chocolate splattered over Olivia's skirt. But Georgia didn't notice; she was too upset. The tears, a bottomless dark lake behind her eyes, spilled over as she shouted, "If it's such a special day, then why won't you be there? If you really wanted to give me something that mattered, you would come and watch me." She gave a little sob. "But maybe I'm not as important as your horrible job."

"Georgia, you know there are going to be two redundancies in the department. I've got to go in today or I'll be the first for the chop. . ." cried the woman, but Georgia was gone, already out of the door, her bag in hand, and scurrying across the road towards the Swan, only just avoiding a red bus and several large puddles in her blind rush. She disappeared into the throng of people making their way through the front gate.

Nobody in the café said anything; there was just a terrible embarrassed silence. The woman gathered up her belongings and put the ring back into its box in her pocket. She looked sad and tired, thought Olivia, as if her daughter's words had punched her in the stomach and knocked all the stuffing out of her. Olivia gave her a little smile, but the woman just shook her head wearily and hurried out of the door.

"Right," said Jack, watching the people making their way up the steps towards the sliding glass door of the Swan. "Time we got this circus on the road, chicks." They stepped out on to the pavement, moving towards the kerb, and as they did so a large black four-by-four with tinted windows drew up right in front of them, splashing straight through a puddle. Muddy water spattered all over them. The driver of the car, a big man in a shiny sleek suit, leapt out. For a moment Olivia thought he was going to apologise to them, but instead he ignored them entirely, strode round to the other side of the car and opened the door.

"Come along, kitten, or you're going to be late, and that would never do." A pretty girl, dressed like a dancer, with long blonde hair so sleek and straight it looked as if every single strand had been individually ironed, emerged from the car holding a large red vanity case.

"She looks like a princess," whispered Eel, deeply impressed.

"Have you got everything, Katie?" asked the man.

The girl raised her eyebrows to the heavens. "Course I have, Dad."

"Good girl," said her father. "Off you go. Your mum and I will be in the front row, cheering our little star on."

The girl looked pensive. "I've told you before, Dad, I'm in the chorus; I haven't got a solo."

"Well, it's a crime. You should have a solo, kitten. My girl is the best. You know, I might even have a word with the old Swan. What was she thinking of, choosing that mousy Georgia Jones over you?"

"Don't say anything, Dad," said Katie. "It won't help, you know what she's like." She put on a prissy voice and said, "Success in this business is not just about talent, Katie, it's about dedication, hard work and learning to be part of a team."

"But she's got to be made to understand that you're special, Katie. You're not just any old Swan pupil. My Katie isn't one of the team. You're a star and you're going to shine." He looked hard at his daughter. "What are you, Katie?"

"I'm a star, Dad," said Katie.

"That's right, you're a star. And what are you going to do, kitten?"

"I'm going to shine, Dad, shine," said his daughter, and she tossed her hair and arched her back and gave a little smile that made her look like a pampered cat.

"That's my girl," said the man. "Off you go now, and remember show business is a cut-throat business. All those other girls in your class, they aren't your friends, they're your rivals. I didn't get where I am today by being nice, and you won't get to be a star unless you beat the competition."

"I know that, Dad," said Katie. "I've wanted to be famous since the day I was born and I'm not going to let anything stop me."

The man watched his daughter approvingly as she entered the Swan and then went to get back into his car. He looked at Olivia, Eel and Jack, who were still wiping away the splattered mud.

"What do you think you're staring at?" he said aggressively, before roaring away and sending spray flying again.

Olivia, Eel and Jack looked at each other, shocked, then they all burst out laughing.

"Stage-school brat," said Eel.

"Stage-school dad," said Jack.

"Well, if either of you turn out like that," said Olivia, "I'll refuse to speak to you ever again."

Chapter Three

Georgia peered through the crack in the red velvet curtains and out into the auditorium of the Swan Academy theatre. It was slowly beginning to fill with people. She knew that she shouldn't be doing it, and Miss Swan would be furious, but she couldn't resist watching as the audience came in. It stopped her thinking about the hurt look on her mum's face for a second.

Today was supposed to be her big day, but now it felt spoiled. She was going to sing one of her favourite songs: "Popular". She'd heard it sung three times by the witch, Galinda, in the musical *Wicked* (once with her mum, who had saved up to give Georgia a Christmas treat, and twice with Katie Wilkes-Cox, sitting in the best seats in the house). She was also going to perform a contemporary dance all on her own. She was the chosen one. Not just a face in the chorus, but a soloist. She hummed the tune and sang a line, changing the lyrics to: "Popular. I wanna be popular. . ."

Georgia knew that she wasn't really popular. Not like Tom McCavity, who was so full of life, or head girl Abbie Cardew, who was looked up to because she was gifted and generous, or even Katie Wilkes-Cox, who wasn't always liked but was admired by most of the girls because she sashayed around giving off a golden aura of talent and self-confidence. She was rich too, buying other people's devotion with a constant stream of free theatre tickets and invitations to parties, barbecues and sometimes even holidays to exotic destinations. She had taken Kylie Morris with her on safari one year, and when they came back Tom McCavity had said it was a pity that both of them hadn't been eaten by lions but then lions probably had better taste than to eat Katie.

Georgia wished she had Katie's easy confidence. She hoped that being chosen to perform a solo would make people see her differently. Not just as the quiet girl who was good at maths and quite good at dancing, singing and acting. She had seen the fleeting looks of envy on the faces of some of the other girls and boys, many of them much older, when Miss Swan had called out her name. It was almost unheard of for someone only just going into Year Eight to be chosen for a proper solo. She was so thrilled that she didn't even mind when Katie Wilkes-Cox had been cold and distant and hadn't invited Georgia to an end-of-term swimming-pool party with all the other girls in the year.

It was worth missing the party for today, thought Georgia, trying to obliterate the memory of the row with her mum. This was her chance to show everybody what she could do. She mustn't let anything ruin it. Even Katie had grudgingly thawed and renewed the friendship, as if hoping that some of Georgia's good fortune would rub off on her. Katie liked to be associated with success. But unlike some of the others, such as Aeysha, Leila and William, who had congratulated Georgia and said she deserved it, Katie had made it quite clear that she thought Miss Swan must have been suffering from some kind of brain meltdown when she had picked

Georgia to perform solo over her.

"I expect she felt sorry for you, cos of your dad leaving you and your mum, and wanted to cheer you up," Katie had said with a toss of her glossy hair. "My dad said it couldn't possibly be for any other reason," she added, with her curious little smile that made her look like a cat that had just swallowed a pint of double cream.

Georgia had tried not to let Katie's words wound her inside. She so desperately wanted to be Katie's friend, because Katie always seemed so cool and confident in a way that Georgia envied.

But Katie could be rather *too* cool and confident. She often acted as though she were superior, and put other people down; said one thing to people's faces and quite another behind their backs. She told Leila Melita that she loved her style of dancing, but told everyone else that Leila looked like a knock-kneed giraffe. Even so, very few of the girls turned down the opportunity to be part of Katie's chosen circle, not even Shannon, who was kind to everyone, and Aeysha, who seldom said a nasty word against anyone.

Once when they were alone together, shortly after Katie had remarked loudly that Aeysha's new coat made her look like a woolly mammoth, Georgia had asked Aeysha why it was that they still clustered around Katie even when she was often so nasty. Georgia had thought Aeysha would say it was for the invitations to snazzy restaurants or paintballing trips, but Aeysha had thought for a moment and then said it was because hanging around Katie made you feel more alive. You could never predict how she would behave and whether she would offer her friendship or withdraw it, and that made her exciting.

"It's as if Katie is the bright light, and we're the moths fluttering around her, trying to get as close as possible without being burned," said Aeysha.

Georgia, who would never have thought to say something like that, decided that Aeysha was probably right. But she had to keep reminding herself that *she* was the one that Miss Swan had chosen, not Katie. Katie's words swirled around her brain; maybe she was right and Georgia had been chosen out of kindness or pity and not because she had real talent. She half expected that at any minute Miss Swan would appear in a flurry of green velvet and announce that it had all been a mistake and that she had never meant for Georgia to do a solo.

She had a sherbety fizzing feeling in her tummy. She always did when she was about to perform. It was like feeling a little bit sick but also excited at the same time. The sort of feeling that you got on a really thrilling fairground ride. She peered out again, hoping against hope that her mum might have decided to come after all and that she would spot her sitting on one of the shabby red-velvet seats, smiling in anticipation of watching Georgia perform. But of course she wasn't there, she was at work trying to cling on to her job and make sure that they didn't fall another month behind with the mortgage. Georgia thought it was horrible having to count every penny; why couldn't they be rich like Katie?

"Georgia Jones, stop that at once. You know that it's unprofessional to peep through the curtains!" It was Abbie Cardew. Georgia jumped back guiltily and turned around to smile at Abbie. Everyone said that the head girl was the most talented student at the school; she had already starred in a West End revival of *Annie* and played the young Jane Eyre on TV. Georgia's only professional jobs so far had been in the chorus of a pantomime and playing a singing strawberry in a TV advert for fruit yogurts. She wished she could get more work so she could pay her own school fees and save her mum all the worry. She loved her mum and hated to see her so anxious all the time. She wanted to bring a smile to her face. She waited until Abbie went to help do the make-up of some of the younger children, and then she risked one last peep through the curtains. You never knew, maybe her mum would be there after all.

Chapter Four

It was the first day of the autumn term at the Swan Academy, and the theatre auditorium was filling up fast with the new intake of children talented enough to get through the long, demanding audition process. Some people said that it was harder to get into the Swan than it was to break into the vaults of the Bank of England and that you were more likely to win the lottery than a place at the school. For those who survived the auditions (in which they had to sing, dance and perform a speech from a classic play), the call-back and then the weekend workshop (during which the final selections were made), it did indeed feel as if they had won a golden ticket. Alicia Swan always said that the audition process was long and intense because she wasn't looking for children who were good at showing off, but for those who still had no idea of the depth of their talent and own potential. The time you were most likely to spot those children was when they weren't acting or singing or dancing, but were just being themselves.

An expectant buzz of excitement rose in the theatre where the new children and their parents sat, and nobody took any notice of two shabby girls – one pale and serious, her dark curtain of hair almost covering her face, and a younger one with crazy chestnut ringlets and mischievous sparkling hazel eyes – slipping into the back row of the theatre, accompanied by an even shabbier-looking man.

Nobody that is except Georgia, who immediately recognised them as the children from the café. She thought she had heard the older one call the younger one Eel, but that seemed unlikely. Surely nobody would call their child Eel? They were a strange little group with their patched clothes and battered luggage. Georgia wondered why they had brought suitcases with them and what the wire, trailing from the biggest case, could possibly be for?

The smaller girl was fidgeting around in her seat while her hand was being firmly held by her older sister as if she was a baby, but she looked at least seven, maybe eight. The older girl lifted her head and pushed back her curtain of hair. She was really striking, thought Georgia. Not obviously pretty but with the pale, serious face of a figure in a medieval painting. The girl shifted and whispered something to her little sister. Both children looked up and seemed to be staring directly at Georgia. The sharp-eyed younger girl grinned cheekily and stuck her tongue out. Georgia, who hadn't thought that anyone could possibly spot her, blushed and withdrew quickly. There was something unsettling about the children's gaze. Georgia felt flustered.

"OK, little Miss Georgia Jones?" asked Katie, who had crept up behind Georgia without her hearing. Katie was her understudy; if for some reason Georgia couldn't go on, it would be Katie who would take her place in the programme. "Are you quite sure that you're going to be able to perform?"

"Quite sure, thank you," said Georgia very politely. "I'm cool." She told Katie about the strange-looking children. Katie peered through the curtain. Eel stuck out her tongue at her too.

"They don't look like the sort of kids who should be at this school. Miss Swan must be letting her standards slip," announced Katie snobbishly. She smiled her cat-like smile. "We'll have to teach those two some manners when classes begin tomorrow. But, Georgia, I'm really not sure you should perform today. You look very pale, as if you might faint at any minute. You only ever get one chance like this; you don't want to blow it. P'r'aps you should tell Miss Swan that you can't go on."

Much to Georgia's relief, at that moment Abbie returned."Off you go, Katie," she said. "Only soloists are allowed here. Go back to the Green Room with the rest of the chorus, where you belong." It was said entirely without malice, but Abbie's thoughtless phrasing had an electrifying effect upon Katie, who tossed her head and glowered. But at that moment a call came over the tannoy for Abbie to return to the dressing rooms to help Miss Hanbury with the costumes. As soon as Abbie was out of sight, Georgia peeped through the curtains again. She wanted to have one last look for her mum.

Katie watched Georgia's back, her cheeks blazing. Abbie's words had been like a punch in her stomach, brutal and direct. She could hardly breathe with rage. It was *so unfair*! It should be her, not Georgia, who was doing a solo. Well, she would show them all who was the really gifted one. Her dad was right, if people were too stupid to recognise your talent, you had to fight your way to the top on your own. She would do everything that was necessary to become a star, starting right now.

She took a step towards Georgia. It was so very tempting. She took a quick look around. Nobody was there to see. Katie raised her hands and shoved Georgia in the small of the back as hard as she could. With a surprised yelp, Georgia shot through the curtains and tumbled off the stage into a heap on the floor of the auditorium, twisting her ankle. From her place behind the curtains, Katie heard the audience gasp, then several people called for help. But she didn't hang around to see what happened next. Instead, she sauntered casually back to the Green Room, all the while whistling the tune of "Popular". Once there, she mingled with the crowd as if she had never been anywhere else.

In the auditorium, Olivia saw Georgia shoot through the curtain like a ball blasted out of a cannon; she rushed helter-skelter down the steps towards the stage to help her. Georgia lay on her back, her foot twisted at an awkward angle. A single tear glistened on her cheek.

"It was my big chance. I was going to do a solo. I wanted to make my mum really proud of me," she whispered. "She'll be so disappointed. I'm glad she wasn't here to see me like this." Olivia squeezed Georgia's clammy hand.

"You'll get other chances," said Olivia kindly. "And I bet your mum's already proud of you; she must be if you were chosen to do a solo." But Georgia had closed her eyes and Olivia was moved aside by the arrival of Sebastian Shaw, the acting teacher, and India Taylor, the senior dancing teacher, who gently pulled Georgia to her feet and helped her limp away.

As they moved off, Olivia overheard Sebastian ask Georgia how the accident had happened. A look of confusion mixed with dismay crossed Georgia's face.

"I don't know," she said miserably. "Somebody . . . no." She shook her head, which felt a bit fuzzy. "I must've slipped. One minute

I was peeping out of the curtains and the next I was on the floor in front of the stage."

Miss Taylor tutted. "Accidents do happen, and that's why there are rules about not looking through the curtains. In any case it is very unprofessional. You really are a silly girl, Georgia, and you've only yourself to blame."

Olivia looked after them thoughtfully. She had seen Georgia careering through the curtain at high speed and it didn't look to her as if she'd slipped. It had looked very much to Olivia as if Georgia had been pushed. She wondered who had done it, and why.

Chapter Five

It took a while for the auditorium to quieten down after the excitement of Georgia's accident but soon every seat was taken and the audience waited expectantly, ready for the show to begin. The Swan school term properly started the next day when every child would turn up in the distinctive olive-green and gold uniform, with all the changes of clothing needed for a day not just of normal lessons but also classes in jazz, tap, ballet, singing, acting and more. Swan children could always be spotted on the bus and Tube, not just by their uniforms but by the sheer amount of stuff they were carrying, and by the fact they were often trying to learn lines or studying a musical score. Being at the Swan was fun, but immensely hard work too.

But today was a day for celebration and everyone was wearing their own clothes. In just a few minutes the new children and their families would be treated to a school tradition: a performance by the current pupils especially dedicated to the "newbies", as the newcomers were known. Being part of the newbies' concert was considered a great honour.

Then there would be a welcoming speech by the school's legendary owner, Alicia Swan. Her own spectacular career in musical theatre had been cruelly cut short by the arthritis that gnarled her beautiful hands and twisted her feet so that she now walked with a stick. Since then she had devoted herself to nurturing "the stars of the future" and so far she was making an excellent job of it. Newspapers called Alicia "the star-maker". She could sniff out talent just like a terrier could smell a rat. Her own daughter, Antonia Swan, had been acclaimed the greatest classical actress of her generation – she was a heart-breaking Ophelia in *Hamlet,* a brilliant Viola in *Twelfth Night,* a luminous Rosalind in *As You Like It,* a Juliet to die for in *Romeo and Juliet* – before she fell head over heels in love with a high-wire daredevil and abandoned her glittering career to run away and join a circus. Alicia had found it hard to forgive Toni, but, after several years of estrangement, mother and daughter had been reconciled. Toni had been on the brink of making a comeback on the West End stage playing Antigone when she had been killed in a plane crash on her way to the first day of rehearsals.

There was barely a West End or Broadway show that didn't have a former Swan student in it. Hollywood's highest-paid heart-throb, Theo Deacon, was a Swan boy, and since its first appearance in the Saturday night schedules, the UK's most successful TV talent show, *You're a Star!*, had been dominated by ex-Swan pupils. The show's producer and chief judge, Robert Howell, had laughingly threatened to ban anyone with connections with the school.

Swan students had been selected to appear in the annual Children's Royal Spectacular at the London Palladium more times than any other stage school. But this year there was a change in the selection process and the line-up of those appearing in front of the Queen would be voted for by the TV-viewing public in a live knockout competition. The Swan would be fighting for its place in the final line-up against the strongest teams from the best stage schools, youth theatre and dance groups in the country.

Alicia was confident that the Swan boasted enough talent to see them through. She had high hopes for the new intake; there were some exceptionally gifted boys and girls among them. She knew that somewhere in the theatre today there were some real stars in the making. Often it was the quiet ones who surprised you most.

Chapter Six

The lights went down, the music soared and Alicia Swan appeared on stage in a halo of light. She welcomed everybody warmly and announced that there would be a slight change to the programme: Katie Wilkes-Cox would be replacing Georgia Jones to sing the well-known song "Popular" and perform a dance. She took a gracious bow, acknowledged the rousing applause of her staff and current students who were ranged behind her on the stage, their faces shining, and then made her way down to her seat in the front row.

Alicia was an elegant and glamorous figure dressed in dark-green velvet whose delicate movements didn't betray the pain and effort of every step she took. Her hand reached into her pocket and she gave an imperceptible sigh as she felt the creased letter that had arrived that morning. Like all the previous letters she had sent, this one had arrived back at the school with the words "Return to sender. Addressee unknown" stamped across the front.

The band played again, and in the back row Eel tossed her chestnut ringlets and squirmed furiously.

"Stop it, Eel," said Olivia.

"I can't help it, Livy. It's the music, it makes me want to dance. It's as if my feet have taken on a life of their own like that girl in *The Red Shoes*."

Olivia clutched her little sister's hand even more tightly as rows of tap-dancing children took to the stage in a spectacular song-and-dance sequence that soon had the audience cheering wildly.

Eel watched fascinated, tapping her feet in perfect time, although she had never had dancing lessons. She longed to be up there on the stage. She thought it must be wonderful to have everyone looking at you. The tap dancers were replaced by a cheeky-faced boy and a girl who did a version of "I'd Do Anything" from

Oliver! The girl was charming, and the boy, who had red hair and freckles, made the audience laugh.

Alicia watched with approval. Aeysha Aziz and Tom McCavity would both go far. Tom's mix of bashfulness and cheek made the audience feel warm and smiley, as if they were toasting their toes in front of a cosy fire.

Under cover of the clapping Olivia leaned towards her father, and as she did so she noticed the worry lines around his tired, handsome face and the dark shadows under his eyes.

"I thought," she whispered, "you were going to introduce us to our grandmother, not take us to see a show." Jack Marvell shifted in his seat uncomfortably. The truth suddenly dawned on Olivia and she gazed at him hard with her piercing green eyes. "She does actually know that we're coming, doesn't she? You did phone her and ask her if it would be all right if we all moved in with her for a while?"

Guilt flickered across Jack Marvell's pale, weary face. "Actually, I decided it might be better if I didn't. I'm not Alicia Swan's favourite person. She blames me for taking your mother away from her and the glory of the London stage, and holds me responsible for Toni's death too. The last time I saw Alicia was at your mother's funeral and she said that she never wanted to see me again. I took her at her word. She seemed very certain about it. I think she feels that if Toni hadn't run away to join the circus with me in the first place, she would never have been on that plane."

He looked drawn and sad. Jack Marvell seldom talked about his wife's death. It was too painful for him, and Olivia and Eel had learned not to ask about Toni. But not talking about her mother made it feel to Olivia as if everybody was trying to pretend that Toni had never existed. Eel was still a baby and Olivia had been only five when her mum had died, and when she tried to remember her face everything became a little hazy. Mostly she could just remember her mum's smell, a hint of lily of the valley.

When she was little there had been photographs of her mother everywhere in their caravan, often captured by the great theatre photographers while playing her most famous roles. But after she had died the photographs had disappeared, as if Jack could not bear to be reminded of what he had lost or of anything to do with the theatre. Jack had plunged himself into work, but sometimes at night, when he thought the children were fast asleep, Olivia had seen him take one of the photos from his box of precious things and stare at it so hard it seemed as if he was trying to will Toni back to life. Marisa, the tattooed circus contortionist who could squeeze her entire body into a small suitcase, had once told Olivia that her parents' relationship had been a real love affair. "They were like Romeo and Juliet."

"So," said Olivia hotly, forgetting to lower her voice, "we're going to be a horrible surprise for her then." People turned round in the rows in front and *sssh*ed them angrily.

A girl and boy who had been doing a *pas de deux* from *Swan Lake* were applauded and replaced by the girl Olivia recognised from the four-by-four. The music began and Katie's clear voice filled the auditorium, pure and sweet.

"Whenever I see someone
Less fortunate than I
(And let's face it – who isn't
Less fortunate than I?)
My tender heart
Tends to start to bleed..."

"I can't believe you've done this to us," hissed Olivia.

"I'll explain," said Jack desperately. People glared at them.

"And when someone needs a makeover
I simply have to take over
I know I know exactly what they need
And even in your case
Tho' it's the toughest case I've yet to face
Don't worry – I'm determined to succeed
Follow my lead
And yes, indeed
You will be:

Popular!"

"We're hardly going to be very popular with our grandmother! She won't want us and you clearly don't want us either," said Olivia loudly. People all around gave them thunderous looks of disapproval. Jack Marvell beckoned desperately to Olivia and Eel and the three of them slipped out of the theatre and into the foyer with Olivia still holding tightly on to Eel's hand.

Katie was just reaching the end of the song.

"La la la la
You'll be popular
Just not quite as popular
As me!"

Chapter Seven

"Olivia," said Jack quietly, and Olivia thought she heard a crack in his voice, "you know that you are not unwanted. You and Eel are the most wanted children in the world. You two are all I've got left, you're my reason for living. But I'm just not able to look after you on my own at the moment. When I can, I will. I promise. The Great Marvello never breaks a promise."

"I know that," said Olivia fiercely and she did. Her father was a man of his word. After his accident had stopped him performing and audiences had dwindled away to nothing, he desperately tried to keep the circus together, paying all the other performers week after week, and it was this generosity that had got them into the trouble they were in now. Because it was the

Great Marvello – the infamous high-wire walker who had skipped across the top of Niagara Falls and fearlessly negotiated the chasm between the two highest points in Paris, even stopping on the wire to light a Primus stove and fry an egg – who everybody wanted to see. But he couldn't perform because he had broken both his legs and four ribs in an accident in a small town in Italy, just one of the many stops the circus made as it endlessly travelled across Europe and the further-flung parts of Scotland and Ireland.

Olivia felt sick whenever she thought about that bright January morning that had begun so full of promise but had almost ended in tragedy. They had been walking down the main street on the way back from the market. Eel skipped along a few metres in front of Olivia and Jack, as always moving as if she was responding to some invisible orchestra playing inside her head. Jack was talking intently to his elder daughter, shyly proposing that they might start trying to work up a tightrope double act together.

"You've come on so well, Liv. You're improving every day. It would be fun to work together, and a father–daughter double act could be a real draw, something a bit different."

Olivia was thrilled. She and Eel had always done bits and bobs to help out in the circus, selling the tickets and programmes, helping the performers do their quick costume changes and joining in the finale with some acrobatics, but this was different. Her dad was asking her to be his partner. He must think that she was genuinely good. High-wire walking was dangerous and if you worked with a partner, you had to trust that person completely. It was essential, because your lives were in each other's hands.

Olivia felt as if she had swelled to twice her normal size with pride. She opened her mouth to say "yes", when she saw a look of horror on her father's face. Eel had skipped her way into the road, entirely oblivious to the car that was racing towards her. Jack lunged at Eel, knocking her out of the way. There was a screech of brakes and a sickening thud. A bag of tomatoes had split, and its contents oozed all over the tarmac. Jack lay very still in the road. For a few moments there had been an eerie silence and then from somewhere far away came the sound of an ambulance siren.

The driver of the speeding car was shaken but unhurt, Eel escaped entirely unscathed and everyone said that it was a miracle Jack had survived the impact. But the bones had been slow to heal, and sometimes Olivia wondered whether her father had broken something even more precious in the accident: his spirit.

From behind the doors of the auditorium they heard a racket of applause. There was a pause and then the music swelled again.

"What if Granny Alicia simply turns us away?" asked Olivia nervously, grasping Eel's hand more firmly.

"She won't," said Jack. "Alicia may be a bit of a dragon, but she has a kind heart. It's just that her daughter's death broke it. Once she's met you, she won't refuse to help you. You are her granddaughters, her daughter's children. Flesh and blood. She won't turn you away and let you starve. I know she'll take you in."

"Take *us* in," said Olivia slowly. "But what about you?" The shifty look once again flashed across Jack's face. "You're not intending to stay with us, are you?" Olivia shouted, furious. "You're planning to dump Eel and me on a grandmother we've never met and who probably won't be at all pleased to see us and then you're going to run away, aren't you, leaving us at this awful place, *a stage school,* knowing full well that neither of us can sing, dance or act so it will be hell for both of us. You couldn't have made a worse job of it if you really *had* found an orphanage run by a wicked witch."

"Liv, it's not like that, honestly," cried Jack despairingly, and he would have gone on but at that moment they both realised that Eel was no longer holding Olivia's hand. Olivia looked around wildly and ran to the big glass doors that led to the busy road, expecting at any moment to hear another ominous screech of brakes. Could Eel have slipped outside without them noticing? Then she heard an outraged shriek from inside the auditorium. Olivia and her father looked at each other and rushed back inside the theatre.

Chapter Eight

Katie had always known that one day she would be famous. It wasn't a question of *if*, just *when*. For somebody with her talent and looks, it was guaranteed. She felt certain of that. Today was the start of the journey that would eventually take her to starring roles and the front covers of all the glossy magazines. She'd shine in the West End and on Broadway and she'd make movies and win a Best Actress Oscar while still in her teens. Her acceptance speech would be so humble and moving that it would reduce all who saw it to helpless tears and become iconic on YouTube. She thought it must be lovely to have people waiting outside your house day and night, wanting to take photos of you.

Her stomach was fizzing like a firework but

as soon as she stepped on stage into the light, all her nerves evaporated. This was what she was born to do. She was a natural. Others might need long hours of practice in the rehearsal room, but not her, not Katie Wilkes-Cox. She opened her mouth and the clear notes rose into the air like balloons. She began to enjoy herself. She couldn't see the audience, but she could feel them. She thought of the audience as being like a big cat, and by singing the song really well she was tickling the cat's tummy and making it purr. She could feel the cat eating out of her hand, coming back greedily for more.

The song was a huge success and the audience roared their approval. Katie beamed and bowed and felt as if she might burst with excitement. She saw Georgia sitting in the front row, very pale, with her ankle bandaged. For a split second Katie felt a twinge of guilt, but then she remembered what her dad had said. Georgia wasn't a friend, she was a rival. Her dad was always right. After all, he had made millions through his property-developing business. He was a success, and Katie wanted to be successful just like him.

She sneaked a glance towards Miss

Swan. She was looking at Katie with a look of amusement on her face. Katie took that for approval. She had shown the old Swan that she was a real star and that she should have picked her in the first place. Katie allowed her mind to drift for a moment as she acknowledged the applause. The audience loved her. She imagined Miss Swan tapping her on the shoulder afterwards and leading her into her snug office, settling her down in one of the comfy armchairs with the paisley throws, offering her apple juice and chocolate biscuits, before leaning forward and saying, "Katie, my dear, you are a very, very special girl, undoubtedly the most supremely talented child that we have ever had at the Swan, and I intend to devote myself to turning you into a massive star. From now on you will have my full attention."

Katie was so enjoying her fantasy that she almost missed the opening bars of the music for her dance. She had to concentrate. She took the first few steps. She was very conscious of her body and of the fact that she had to coax it into doing what she wanted. She knew that, unlike Georgia, she didn't have great technique. But Katie was sure that she had something much more important: natural flair. Practice was for the also-rans like Georgia, not for real stars like her. She relaxed a little as the music seeped into her brain; she felt the audience beginning to relax too. She took several more steps, then she prepared to make an impressive leap. She left the ground, momentum carried her through the air and then she bumped into something and gave an outraged shriek. What was going on? She was supposed to have the stage all to herself, but there was somebody else there, a small child with crazy chestnut ringlets who was doing a mad dance to the music, occasionally throwing in a cartwheel or an astonishing back flip. The orchestra played on.

Rushing back into the auditorium, Olivia and Jack stood transfixed with horror as they watched Eel fling herself energetically around the stage as if she'd been performing all her life. They stared at each other, aghast. Olivia looked around the audience, which seemed confused by the appearance of this newcomer, but also deeply impressed. Several people were looking at their programmes trying to work out who she was. Eel did a back flip and the audience cheered wildly, then she started to do a pretend tap dance and was so funny that the audience laughed loudly, and one little boy even fell off his seat.

Jack smiled, but Olivia was in agonies. Eel was being *so* embarrassing. She wanted to leap on to the stage and pull her sister off, take her by the hand and run out of the building and keep running all the way back to Italy. But Jack, who in a split second had decided that intervention would be even more disruptive, put a calming hand on her shoulder. Eel did an explosive series of cartwheels and the audience erupted, some even rose to their feet.

Katie looked wildly around. This was her one big chance and she was being well and truly upstaged! What's more, it was by that nasty, rude little girl who had stuck her tongue out at her. She was furious and felt deeply humiliated. When the audience laughed at Eel's cheeky tap-dancing, she felt they were laughing at her. This couldn't be happening! Not to her, not to Katie Wilkes-Cox, the coolest girl at the Swan. She longed for a winged monster to sweep down from the ceiling and carry Eel away in its talons. She stopped dancing, marched over to the child, seized her by her chestnut ringlets and started trying to drag her off the stage.

"No!" cried Olivia, running down the steps towards the stage with Jack just behind her. The audience gasped and murmured, creating a low-level buzz, because one child pulling another by the hair couldn't possibly be part of the show. The school orchestra, which had been taught to play on whatever the circumstances, faltered and stopped. The entire auditorium fell eerily silent.

Katie pulled Eel over and Eel screamed. "Get off the stage, you little horror! Get off!" shouted Katie. "You've ruined my big moment. I'll teach you to upstage me. You'll wish that you'd never been born by the time I've finished with you. Nobody upstages me. Particularly not some talentless little kid like you who can't even dance properly!"

A ripple of astonishment passed through the audience. Olivia felt some satisfaction as a few people booed. Some in the audience were clearly rather enjoying the spectacle; others could hardly bear to look at the stage. In seconds, Olivia and Jack had reached the bottom of the stairs. As they did so, Katie's dad rose from his front-row seat, his face screwed up in rage, and started to clamber awkwardly on to the stage, a murderous glint in his eye.

"No!" shouted Olivia again. She had to save her little sister!

Chapter Nine

"Katie Wilkes-Cox, let go of that child at once!" Alicia Swan's voice cut across the auditorium like a knife. Olivia skidded to a halt on the steps. Katie let go of Eel's hair. She still felt as if she might explode with anger, but she could hear the icy disapproval in Miss Swan's voice. It was as if somebody had thrown a bucket of cold water over her. The fire inside her burned away to ashes and she stood frozen to the spot. Eel wriggled beside her, not in the least embarrassed but feeling slightly surprised to find herself there at all. She couldn't remember running on to the stage; it was as if she had been bewitched by the music.

Alicia Swan made her way on to the stage. Her impressive presence immediately quietened the audience. She calmly addressed Katie's dad. "Mr Wilkes-Cox, do please go back to your seat." For a moment he looked as if he might be about to argue, but there was such authority in Alicia's tone that he suddenly deflated and shuffled back to his seat like an oversized toddler who has just been scolded by his mum.

"I apologise for this unforeseen spectacle," said Alicia graciously, adding with a wry smile, "but sometimes the impromptu can be the most revealing, and it is when something unexpected happens that you make the most important discoveries." The audience suddenly relaxed. Alicia had such a commanding presence that all potential for embarrassment passed and they leaned forward in their seats, completely absorbed in what was unfolding. It felt as if something momentous was about to happen.

Alicia turned to Eel and studied her face intently. "What's your name, my dear?" she asked kindly.

"Eel."

Alicia raised an eyebrow. "And are you one of the new children?" she enquired, although she knew that she would remember this child if she had seen her before at the auditions. Eel shook her head.

"Perhaps you are the little sister of a boy or girl who is starting at the school this term?"

Eel shook her head again. She liked this lady; she seemed very kind, not at all as Jack Marvell had described. "My dad says that you are a bit fierce, but he's the wrongest he's ever been because you don't seem such a dragon." The audience laughed. There was something charming about this wild child. Even Miss Swan smiled.

"Well, I do try not to breathe fire," she agreed. "Eel, you dance very well. You have a gift for it. Would you like to come to my school and we'll teach you how to do it properly?" Eel nodded vigorously, her ringlets bouncing up and down.

"But that's not fair!" shouted Katie, unable to contain herself. "She's being rewarded for ruining my big chance—"

She was silenced by a look from Miss Swan, who turned back to Eel. "Now, point out your parents and I'll talk to them after the show."

"I don't have a mum. She died," said Eel, "but my dad and sister are there." She pointed towards the auditorium where Olivia and Jack stood in the semi-darkness. "We wanted to see you anyway because Dad says my sister is going to come here as well. So we'll all be together."

Alicia looked very confused. "Does he indeed?" she said.

"He does. All the time," said Eel firmly. She held out her hand towards a rather flummoxed Alicia to formally introduce herself. "I'm Alicia Ophelia Rosalind Marvell, but everyone calls me Eel, and you are my grandmother. That," said Eel, pointing to the stairs, "that's my big sister, Livy. Olivia Viola Juliet Marvell." Worried that Alicia wasn't quite keeping up, Eel added, "She's your granddaughter too."

The audience gasped; the events unfolding on stage could hardly be more dramatic. It was like a final scene by Shakespeare when the characters are all unexpectedly reunited and people discover their long-lost relatives. Alicia's eye followed Eel's finger to where Jack and Olivia were standing at the bottom of the gangway. The follow-spot operator suddenly picked them out so they were bathed in light. Olivia froze as if she had been caught in a searchlight and was about to be shot. Alicia's gaze lit upon Olivia's serious, anxious face and for a moment her grandmother thought she'd seen a ghost. She felt dizzy and her eyes filled with tears.

Her eyes met Jack's.

"Hello, Alicia," he said quietly, raising a hand in greeting. Alicia stared at him for a moment, then looked at Eel, who had slipped off the stage and was now hugging Olivia and Jack tightly, and smiled. She took a deep breath and said, "Later, my dears. We'll sort this tangled web out after the performance. I promise."

She clapped her hands and turned to the audience. "You have been waiting patiently and we mustn't disappoint you. You came to see a show and you'll get one, the best the Swan has ever delivered!" She nodded to the band, and then turned to Katie with a kind smile. "From the top of the dance, my dear," she said gently. "You were doing very well before you spoiled it."

"Before *I* spoiled it!" spluttered Katie. She hadn't invaded the stage uninvited, it was that crazy child.

Miss Swan put a finger to her lips, speaking quietly so nobody else could hear. "One thing any truly great performer has to learn, Katie my dear, is how to share the spotlight, not hog it. It's not just about talent, it's about generosity too." Then she clapped her hands again. "The show must – and will – go on!"

Chapter Ten

As soon as the concert was over, everyone crowded into the school hall for refreshments. There were glasses of wine for the parents and juice for the children, and the senior boys and girls carried around trays of food: miniature sausage rolls and quiches; tiny éclairs and fruit tartlets. Georgia and Aeysha had found a corner where they could watch people coming in. Parents were quietly congratulating their children on a good show. It would certainly go down in Swan history as one of the most memorable.

Katie swanned in as if she had just made her triumphant debut on Broadway, not behaved badly at a school concert. A few of the parents looked askance at her, but Katie didn't appear to notice and soon she was swept up in the booming congratulations of her parents, who gave her a large bouquet of flowers and took photos of her. Some of the other parents moved away a little.

"Smile, kitten. I want a picture of my star!" said Katie's dad, elbowing Abbie out of the way. Abbie was carrying a tray of full glasses and only just regained her balance in the nick of time. Encouraged by her mum, Katie pouted for the camera.

"That's my girl!" said Katie's dad. "You were brilliant, kitten, despite that awful kid trying to ruin everything."

Georgia and Aeysha watched the scene from a distance.

"You have to give it to her," said Aeysha. "That girl's got some nerve. If I'd behaved like that I'd want the earth to swallow me whole."

"If it was my mum, she wouldn't be taking pictures, she'd be telling me how ashamed she was of my behaviour," said Georgia, remembering how, a few months after she arrived at the Swan, she'd got so overexcited and nervous at an audition for a TV advert for washing powder that she'd started showing off and had been cheeky to the casting director. She'd thought it was a grown-up thing to do. Her mum had made their excuses, taken her away and told her how disappointed she was in her daughter. The memory still made Georgia feel hot and pink.

"If the Swan is going to turn you into a show-off, then it's not the school for you," Mrs Jones had said. But her qualms were eased by Alicia, who had given Georgia a gentle but firm talking to and agreed with her mum that there should be no more auditions until Georgia had settled down at school.

"She has real talent, Mrs Jones," said Alicia, "and talent is a delicate thing. I couldn't live with myself if it was spoiled by anything we did here at the Swan. But it's the home that really counts. I've seen too many children whose potential has been destroyed by pushy parents thinking their child is a shooting star. The trouble with shooting stars is that they burn out quickly and all you're left with is ash. But you seem remarkably sensible, Mrs Jones, and I'm sure we can work together to realise Georgia's considerable talent and increase her confidence without ruining her. I suspect it was nerves that made her behave the way she did and I also suspect she will have taken the lesson to heart."

Georgia had never been cheeky again and now knew the importance of behaving professionally at all times. Well, almost all; the exception was peeping through curtains before a show!

"How's the ankle?" asked Aeysha sympathetically.

"Not too bad, but there's no way I could've danced on it."

"It's a shame," said Aeysha. "You'd have been ace, much better than Katie." Georgia felt a warm glow of pleasure seep through her tummy. Aeysha wasn't the kind of girl to say things she didn't mean.

"Nah," she protested. "Katie's the one who'll go far. Everyone says it."

"Mostly Katie herself," said Aeysha with a wry smile. "Look! There's that girl Olivia. She looks a bit lost. Do you think she's going to come to school here with her sister? It would feel weird going to a school run by your gran."

Olivia was standing alone in the throng, feeling out of place. Jack and Eel had gone upstairs to Alicia's flat so that Eel could brush her hair and change her clothes. Olivia looked around at the chattering, laughing adults and children and felt invisible. She caught a glimpse of Katie posing for another picture and saw her gran heading towards Katie's dad, laying a hand firmly on his arm and shaking her head. At that moment, Abbie noticed Olivia and took her over to Georgia and Aeysha.

"This is Olivia," she said, "and this is Aeysha and Georgia."

Olivia smiled shyly at Georgia. "We've already met. Twice."

Georgia blushed. "Thanks for helping me," she said.

"If Olivia comes to school here, you three would be in the same class, so maybe you should get to know each other," said Abbie as she hurried away.

"What's it like here?" asked Olivia.

"Wicked," said Georgia and Aeysha so completely in unison that they both burst out laughing. Georgia continued: "It really is, though. I used to go to an ordinary school and now I don't know how I stood it. All those same dreary lessons day after day!"

"Of course, we have to do all the

ordinary lessons," explained Aeysha. "Maths, English, history, French. But we do them in the morning. Then in the afternoon we do the fun stuff: voice, acting, verse-speaking, ballet, tap, contemporary, modern, jazz, street dance, singing, improvisation. From next year we can even take classes in directing, and devising or writing plays. Or songwriting. I can't wait to do that. It would be awesome to write your own songs."

Olivia sighed. "Don't think it's my sort of thing."

"So what *is* Olivia Marvell's thing?" came a voice. It was Tom McCavity, who had wandered over with a plateful of chocolate éclairs. He was followed by William Todd. "We nicked the tray off Abbie when she put it down to talk to someone," said Tom as he shared them out, grinning cheekily.

Olivia shrugged. "I don't know," she said, afraid to mention high-wire walking. If Granny Alicia loathed the circus as much as Jack said she did, maybe everyone at the Swan hated it too. She didn't want them to think she was a total freak. She thought hard.

"Maybe gymnastics," she said shyly,

thinking her acrobatic skill might make her shine there.

"We don't do that here. We don't do any sport. There isn't time," said Georgia sympathetically.

"It's a pain," said Tom. "No football." He made an exaggerated gesture with his hand against his forehead. "I've had to give up the chance to play for Man U for the sake of my art." He pretended to swoon and everyone laughed, even Olivia.

"Playing the idiot as usual, Tom?" said Katie, who had come over to the little group. "When will you ever grow up?" she added witheringly.

"When he's had a few more birthdays," said William. Katie glared.

There was an awkward pause. It was as if Katie was waiting for them all to congratulate her. "It must have been awful for you out there on the stage," blurted out Georgia, to fill the silence. Katie narrowed her eyes and glared at her. Georgia wished she'd kept her mouth shut.

Then Tom went and made things worse. "Everyone's really sorry for you, Georgie girl," he said. "It should have been your big day and

I can't think of anyone who deserved it more. What happened?"

Georgia looked really flustered. She could feel Katie's gimlet gaze. "I really don't know," she stuttered. "I must've slipped."

"It didn't look like you slipped to me. You had far too much momentum," said Olivia, eager to join in the conversation. "From the auditorium side, it definitely looked as if someone pushed you through the curtains."

Georgia's stomach felt as if she'd just been dropped through a trapdoor.

Katie gave a tight little laugh. "Don't be dumb, she slipped. We all know how clumsy Georgia is. It was just bad luck. There's no mystery, just a silly accident. It's her own fault; she shouldn't have been looking through the curtains in the first place." While she said this, Katie held Georgia's gaze very firmly.

Just then, Olivia heard her name being called by Eel. She said goodbye shyly and left.

"She seems nice," said Aeysha.

"I wouldn't count on it," said Katie. "Seems like a bit of a drama queen to me, trying to turn Georgia's stupid accident into some kind of whodunit. And of course," she added casually, "we'll never be able to trust her if she comes to the Swan."

"Why not?" asked Tom.

"Think about it, dummy," said Katie. "She's the Swan's granddaughter. Everything we say or do will go straight back to her old gran. She was probably spying on us just then."

The others shook their heads but a few minutes later Abbie suddenly swooped down on them. "Tom McCavity. I've been looking for you. My spies tell me that it was you and William who stole all the éclairs."

The children stared at each other in surprise.

"There! What did I tell you," said Katie, with her triumphant cat's-got-the-cream smile. "You shouldn't believe a word that Olivia Marvell says. You'll see."

Chapter Eleven

It wasn't until several hours after the newbies' show had finished that Olivia, Eel and Jack had finally been left alone with Alicia. They were in her flat on the top floor of one wing of the school. The living room was dominated by a beautiful portrait of Toni. Olivia couldn't take her eyes off it. It made her feel as if her mother was in the room, looking over them like a guardian angel. Everyone was exhausted, although Eel, who was thrilled at the prospect of being taught to dance, kept saying it was her "bestest day ever".

Olivia decided it was one of her worst days ever, and it showed absolutely no sign of getting any better either. Watching Jack and her grandmother talking was, she thought, a bit like watching two suspicious cats warily circling each other. Alicia, although delighted by her granddaughters' return to London, clearly still blamed Jack for Toni's death. Sensing this, Jack was too proud to tell Alicia that they needed help because they had no money left and nowhere to live.

Eel had fallen asleep on the sofa, a little smile on her face. Olivia curled up beside her with her eyes partially shut, but she was really wide awake and listening. Alicia kept glancing at Olivia and murmuring, "So like her mother," and Olivia overheard her grandmother telling Jack that Eel was one of the most naturally gifted dancers she had ever encountered.

"She needs to dance," said Alicia. "I've come across children like Eel before. Once she's doing what she was born to do, she'll settle down. She's clearly very bright, Jack, and very self-possessed. She just needs an outlet to express herself. Trust me."

She glanced over at Olivia. "What's Olivia's special talent?"

Jack looked a little embarrassed. "She's a high-wire walker like me. In fact, one day she'll be far better than I ever was . . . am." He suddenly looked stricken, but Alicia didn't notice, as she was wrestling with her own emotions. If Toni hadn't gone to the circus that night and fallen in love with Jack at first sight, she would have stayed in London near her mother, continued her triumphant career in the theatre and still be alive.

"Well," said Alicia, a tight little edge creeping into her voice, "maybe she could be persuaded into something worthwhile. Toni had many talents, and I'm sure she will have passed them on. I'm confident we can find something else that Olivia's good at besides high-wire walking. We'll have to if she's going to study at the Swan."

On the sofa, Olivia bristled like an angry hedgehog. How dare her grandmother talk in this arrogant way about something that she loved and that she had spent long hours trying to master, something that was thrilling and dangerous! What could be more worthwhile than high-wire walking, which was both a skill and an art, and was part of the greatest show on earth – the circus. All that silly dancing, singing and acting couldn't compare.

"So," said Alicia. "Where are you staying in London? I can see by your suitcases you came straight here. I hope it's not far. The school day is long and tiring enough without having to trek halfway across London."

"Actually, Alicia. . ." Jack paused. Olivia could see his face, so pained and pale, so unlike the laughing, charismatic father he had once been. Alicia raised an eyebrow and waited.

When Jack didn't say anything for a very long time, Alicia sighed.

"I see," she said. "Am I right in thinking that you don't have anywhere to live?"

"I'm afraid you're correct, Alicia." He stood up and started pacing the room in an agitated manner that only exacerbated his limp. "Alicia, we desperately need help. I want you to look after the children for me. I've got to go away and try to make some money. I've got a plan. But for the moment, we're completely destitute. I haven't a penny to my name. Everything I've got in the world is here in these suitcases and everything I love is lying on that sofa."

"It's exactly as I imagined," said Alicia angrily. "This circus business has been the ruin of you and your family. You've always been completely irresponsible, Jack, living hand to mouth and not thinking beyond the next day. I warned Toni what a circus life would be like and, see, it's reduced your own children to poverty. You're not a fit father."

"He is, he *is* a fit father. He's the best father in the whole world!" cried Olivia, springing to her feet with fury. "How dare you say he's not! *You're* not a fit grandmother. You never tried to get in touch with us to check if we were all right. You just abandoned us after Mum died and told Dad you didn't ever want to see him again. Well, that means that you didn't want to see us either. Because the Marvells come as a package. And he's *not* irresponsible. He was hit by a car and couldn't work and *that's* why we haven't got any money!"

Alicia was staring at Olivia, white-faced. Her fingers grazed the letter in her pocket addressed to Jack that had been returned to her only this morning, but she said nothing.

"You're right, Olivia. I haven't done my duty by you. But I intend to from now on. I make you a solemn promise."

"I don't want your promises!" said Olivia. She strode over to Jack, who had sunk into a chair with his face buried in his hands. "Come on, Dad," she said. "We're clearly not welcome here. Let's go."

"I don't want to go," came a little voice. The noise of angry shouting had woken Eel up and she was sitting on the sofa in a daze. "I want to stay and learn to dance. Granny promised me I could." She burst into noisy tears. Jack scooped her up in his arms and carried her away to the bathroom so that the others wouldn't see he had tears in his eyes, too.

Olivia and her grandmother faced each other. "Olivia, please. . ." said Alicia, feeling her granddaughters slipping away from her again, perhaps this time for ever.

Olivia ignored her.

"Olivia," pleaded Alicia. "Tell me about the accident. Please, Olivia, I want to try to understand."

There was something so desperate in the old woman's eyes that Olivia was persuaded to speak. So, reluctantly at first, Olivia told her grandmother about the car accident in Italy. When she had finished, Alicia said, "Poor, poor man. I noticed he's walking with a limp. I know what it's like to be prevented by accident or illness from doing the thing you love most in the world."

Olivia looked at her grandmother's gnarled, claw-like fingers, so damaged by arthritis, and knew at once that Alicia was speaking from the heart.

"But I don't think it's a physical problem," said Olivia slowly.

"What do you mean?"

Olivia took a deep breath. There was something about her grandmother's face that made her think she might understand the enormity of what had happened to Jack.

"Well, Dad's bones eventually knitted together and he felt ready to go back on the wire. Everyone from the circus was there to see him do it and cheer him on as he climbed the tower for the first time one morning some months after the accident."

"So what happened?" asked Alicia.

"He stepped out on to the wire, and everyone cheered. He took a few steps. But almost immediately we knew something was wrong. He just stopped and stood quite frozen in the middle of the high-wire above our heads. He couldn't go forwards and he couldn't go back. It was as if he was paralysed."

"How did he get down again?"

"I climbed up the opposite tower and stepped out on to the wire," whispered Olivia. "I could see the beads of perspiration on his lip and the fear in his eyes, but it was as if my presence broke the spell. He suddenly moved towards me as if there had never been a problem and took my outstretched hand. But I could feel him trembling. He said, 'Clearly I wasn't quite as ready to return as I had thought. Thank you.' Then he walked away. Nobody said anything, but all the other circus performers avoided meeting my eye."

There was a movement behind them. Olivia realised that her father had come back into the room and had been listening. She felt wretched, as if she had been caught betraying a terrible secret.

"It's all right, Liv," said Jack, touching her cheek tenderly. "It's good to face the truth. I've been trying to ignore it, and your grandmother has a right to know why we need her help."

He turned to Alicia.

"There is an old circus saying, Alicia, which is that fear is a jealous mistress and once she has you in her grip, she never lets you go. Well, fear has caught me and is holding me tight. I've lost my nerve."

"Like some actors do with stage fright," whispered Alicia with a little shudder.

Jack nodded sadly. "I've watched Liv practise every day, but I haven't been up there myself since. I can't face the moment of stepping out on to the wire. It feels like a void waiting to swallow me up. Regrettably, there have been consequences. Audiences stopped coming and gradually the other performers drifted away too. I couldn't blame them. Everyone's got to eat. In the end, we found ourselves alone in Italy with no money. It was either Toni's engagement ring or the battered old Big Top that had to go. Of course, there was no contest. I sold the Big Top and we had just enough to get back home to England." Jack held their gazes, then he added fiercely, "But I'm going to defeat my demons and get back on the wire! I promise you, Liv and Eel. I will do it."

He smiled as if he was already thinking what that would feel like, but everyone else in the room had tears sliding down their cheeks.

Chapter Twelve

"Are you sure you won't stay, Jack? There's plenty of room," said Alicia. "I know we have history, and that there has been bad feeling between us, but you really would be very welcome here. You are my son-in-law and the father of my daughter's children. Giving you a home when you most need it is the least I can do."

"It's kind of you, Alicia," replied Jack. "But although my girls need a home, I can't live on your charity. I'd feel useless. I need to go away for a while and try to restore the family fortunes. Besides, it would be too difficult with me here. I love the circus; you hate it. You love the theatre but since Toni's death I find it too painful to watch anyone acting, because I always think how much better Toni would have been in the role. Before long, we'd be falling out again. It would never work. Besides, this place is full of Toni. This is where she grew up. I'd be living with a ghost looking over my shoulder. It's better that I go."

"But *where* will you go?" asked Eel, who had just walked into the room with Olivia.

"I'm going to stay with my old friend, Pablo. He's got a spare room and he's going to help me with my money-making idea."

"What is it?" asked Eel, clinging to his arm.

"It's a secret," smiled Jack. "But who knows, maybe it will make us all millionaires!"

"Cool," said Eel. "I'd like you to be a millionaire and then you can pay me all the pocket money you owe me."

Olivia hadn't really been listening. She was trying to think where she had heard the name Pablo before, but couldn't remember. She was about to ask Jack when Alicia spoke.

"Well, if you think that it's best that you go, that's all settled then. I'll keep the girls here with me." She held out her hand to Jack. "Goodbye, Jack, and good luck. I hope it all works out, I really do from the bottom of my heart. I'll leave you to make your goodbyes and go and call you a taxi."

Alicia was trying to be tactful and allow the children some time alone with their father, but to Olivia it felt as though she was just trying to bundle Jack out of all their lives as quickly as possible.

Their leave-taking with their father was emotional. "Be good for your grandmother, my lovelies," said Jack, "and I'll be back for you as soon as I can."

"Take me with you!" said Olivia. "I can help you. I won't get in the way, I promise."

"Oh, Liv. I wish I could. But I've got to do what I've got to do on my own. The best way you can help me is by staying here with your gran where I know you'll be safe and looked after. It won't be for long, sweetie, I promise," said her father, hugging both his daughters.

Olivia felt rejected.

"When you come back, I'll be the bestest dancer in the whole world!" said Eel.

"Have you asked Alicia where I can practise my high-wire walking?" asked Olivia, clinging to Jack's arm.

"Actually, Liv, I feel I've already asked

enough. Your grandmother has offered you a home and an education. Wait a week or two until you've all got to know each other better and then ask her yourself. When she realises how much it means to you, I'm sure she'll find you somewhere, but I just don't feel I can ask her this very minute. She's already doing so much for us." He saw Olivia's stricken face. "Stick it out, Olivia. Be brave. It won't be for long, and all the things you learn here will be good for your tightrope-walking. A couple of months of rest from it won't do any harm; it might even do you some good."

"A few months' rest hasn't done you any good, has it?" said Olivia furiously. As soon as the words were out, Olivia regretted them, but she couldn't take them back or stop the terrible wounded look flashing across her father's face. He hugged her close to him and kissed her.

"I love you, Liv. I'm trying to make a future for us, a future that Toni would have been proud of. I'm sorry if you feel I've failed you, but I really am doing my best."

Olivia wanted to hug him forever and tell him how much she loved him, but she felt stung by his words, so she turned her face when he bent to give her one final kiss and didn't see how hurt he was or the tear that glistened in his eye.

She stood alone in the living room while Eel went with him down the stairs to the glass front doors. Suddenly Olivia knew she couldn't let her father leave like that. She raced through the endless corridors and down the three flights of stairs to the foyer of the academy, desperate to say she was sorry and to tell him how much she loved him and that she thought he was the bravest man in the world.

She tore out of the doors and stumbled breathlessly down the steps. But she was too late; the taxi was already disappearing around the corner. Olivia felt as if she had been kicked in the stomach, and the pain was worse because she knew it was self-inflicted.

It was only later when she was lying in bed that Olivia remembered who Pablo was. He was Jack's former agent, who had helped him to set up his most famous stunts. Stunts that were very dangerous and required nerves of steel. A little knot of fear settled in Olivia's stomach and took up home there.

Chapter Thirteen

Olivia stood in the middle of the corridor, desperately studying her timetable and feeling as if she was caught in an endlessly revolving door from which there was no escape. Her brain had turned to mush and she couldn't work out if she was supposed to be heading to singing in the Callas Rehearsal Room, musical theatre in the Sondheim Space or ballet in the Pavlova Studio. The Swan was like a rabbit warren spread out over three floors. Trying to find your way around was difficult, and nobody in her class except Georgia and Aeysha had made any attempt to help her. Even Tom McCavity, who had seemed so funny and nice, was now keeping his distance as if she had somehow offended him.

She got out her map. Olivia knew that the theatre, cafeteria and school hall took up the whole of the ground floor of the huge building, but she had been surprised to discover that there were also music practice rooms there. The upper floors were even more warren-like – a mixture of classrooms and rehearsal rooms. Once, walking past an unmarked room, she had heard terrible screams and had rushed in thinking somebody was being murdered, only to discover that the seniors were rehearsing *Macbeth*. She had backed out of the room, red-faced and embarrassed.

She kept turning up in the wrong rooms in the right clothes or the right rooms in the wrong clothes. She didn't really care; she hated every class equally. She didn't mind the morning academic classes so much, but the vocational lessons in the afternoon were hell. Fortunately they were a hell that stopped at 5 p.m. each day when the final bell sounded and the children tumbled wearily but excitedly out of their classes, rubbing their aching muscles and dreaming of their future careers in the theatre.

Olivia wondered whether she might just sneak to the girls' changing room, stay there for the rest of the day and hope nobody missed her, or whether Abbie Cardew or one of the prefects would discover her and send her to class. Abbie, at least, was always kind to her.

Around her swirled children dressed in practice clothes, all heading purposefully towards their next classes, ballet shoes slung over their shoulders and copies of scripts or musical scores tucked under their arms. At the end of the corridor she spotted Eel skipping her way towards a jazz class, talking so animatedly with her new friends she didn't even glance at her forlorn elder sister. Olivia wished that Eel would notice her and run up and take her hand, but she didn't. Olivia was overwhelmed by a sense of grief: she had lost her old life, and her dad, and now she was losing Eel to the Swan and dancing. She had always been the one who had tried to keep her crazy little sister safe, but now it was Olivia who needed someone to hold her hand.

More pupils passed by, including a group of older boys talking loudly about forming a boy band, and another boy, carrying a cello, who stopped for a moment to scan the upcoming auditions board and accidently rested it on Olivia's toe. A gaggle of excited girls pushed past her to join a group of children being taken for a screen test for a remake of *The Railway Children*. Most of the children took no notice of her, but a few nudged each other as they passed. Olivia had already made an impression, and it wasn't an entirely good one.

Things had gone wrong over breakfast on the first day when Alicia was explaining the timetable to her granddaughters.

"You'll be taking all the dance options, Eel," said Alicia, "and I'll also be arranging a number of private classes for you. We'll reassess the situation in a few weeks to see how you're progressing." Eel wriggled about in her chair and beamed happily.

"Now, Olivia," said Alicia, turning to her elder granddaughter. "It's probably best if you follow a more general vocational curriculum until we discover where your talents lie."

"They lie in the circus," said Olivia sulkily. She hadn't slept a wink and felt as edgy as a crocodile in a handbag factory.

"So Jack tells me. But I'm afraid there isn't any circus training at the Swan. It's really not an area in which we have any interest. We're a performing arts school and our students are heading for the legitimate theatre or TV and the movies, not the sawdust ring." Alicia was irritated by Olivia's sulky face and spoke more harshly than she had intended.

She'd spent so many lonely hours fantasising about being reunited with her grandchildren, and had spent so much time and effort trying to track them down. But now they were here, sitting at her breakfast table, Olivia's resentful face just brought back all Alicia's memories of her arguments with her own daughter. For Alicia, whose own career had been brutally cut short by illness rather than choice, her daughter's decision to willingly give up the stage was incomprehensible, and she had never recovered from the shock of waking up one morning to find that Toni had run away to join Jack and the circus, abandoning both her mother and her career. She looked now at Olivia's wan face and memories of Toni came flooding back. She turned away as tears filled her eyes. Even looking at Olivia felt tender and painful.

Olivia watched her grandmother turn her back on her and felt totally bereft. Nobody cared about her or what she wanted; not Eel, who was thrilled to be at the Swan, not Jack, who, after all the talk of partnership, had clearly decided he didn't need her, and definitely not Alicia, who hated the circus and seemed to hold some kind of personal grudge against her, too.

A week later she still felt exactly the same. Jack had been impatient with her on the phone when she had complained about how horrible everything was at the Swan, such as having to do ballet with the seven-year-olds, which was downright humiliating.

"I feel like an elephant in a room full of baby gazelles," she said, but Jack had just laughed and said that elephants were much more interesting creatures than gazelles. Even Eel was unsympathetic when Olivia moaned about the Swan and about how she couldn't practise the high-wire.

"Why don't you just ask Gran if there's somewhere you can practise?"

"She'll only say no," said Olivia, pushing out her bottom lip.

"You don't know until you ask," said Eel patiently.

"I do," said Olivia. "She's made it quite clear that she hates everything to do with the circus and thinks that circus artists are no better than performing sea lions. She even seems to think that the ring is still sawdust. It's not worth the bother."

Eel shook her head. There was no point in arguing with her sister in this mood; she knew from past experience that you just had to wait for the sun to come out again from behind the cloud in Olivia's head.

Standing in the corridor, Olivia turned her timetable round again and realised that she was due in acting. She turned miserably on her heel and headed up the stairs, dragging her feet.

Chapter Fourteen

Olivia slipped into the Wilde Room, hoping that nobody would notice her, and tried to make herself invisible in a corner. The class had begun long ago. Aeysha, Tom and William Todd were acting out a scene from *The Secret Garden*. Olivia had seen the three of them sitting together at lunchtime in the school cafeteria, running over their lines together while they bolted down vegetable risotto. They were taking this performance in front of their twenty-four classmates and Mr Shaw as seriously as if they were acting before an audience of a thousand people in a West End theatre.

Everyone watched them closely. At the end there was a tiny silence and then everyone applauded enthusiastically.

"I really enjoyed that. Thank you," said Sebastian Shaw, before giving the children some notes about their performances. "Don't hurry too much, William; you're inclined to gabble. Good work, Tom. I like the way you use stillness and silence on stage. Aeysha, you need to think a bit harder about how Mary Lennox really feels. She's much more than just a monster; she behaves badly because she's lost everything she loves: family, country, an entire way of life. You've got to find a way of making us understand that all she says and does is informed by that."

He invited the other children to constructively criticise the actors' performances. Sebastian Shaw was always talking about how important it was for actors to learn to be self-critical and said that process began by learning to discuss – but not judge – other people's performances.

Olivia glanced around and caught Georgia looking at her. Most people in the class kept their distance from Olivia, but she often found Georgia looking at her as if she was on the verge of confessing something momentous to her. Olivia turned away without acknowledging her. She liked Georgia and she needed a friend, but she was wary because Georgia was always hanging around on the fringes of a group that had Katie Wilkes-Cox at its glittering centre. Olivia was determined not to have anything to do with a stage-school brat like her.

It was Katie who stood up now and went to the front of the class. She flicked back her hair and then launched into a speech from Shakespeare's *The Tempest.* She was playing Miranda, a young girl who has just witnessed a shipwreck in a terrible storm and is telling her father, Prospero, what she has seen and asking him to use his powers to stop the storm and save the ship's passengers.

"If by your art, my dearest father, you have
Put the wild waters in this roar, allay them."

Olivia watched, and thought about Jack and how the accident had turned their family life upside down and how he had been powerless to do anything about it. If Eel had never run into the road, they'd still be in Italy or maybe in Ireland or Brittany or Cornwall now, and she would be doing a double act with her dad. Instead she was at the stupid Swan Academy watching

Katie Wilkes-Cox pretending to be somebody else. Not very well, in Olivia's opinion. Katie, thought Olivia suddenly, wasn't being Miranda, she was *acting* being Miranda. Rather too loudly and slightly hysterically. It was false, like everything else at the Swan, thought Olivia, who hated the fact that everyone was so bright-eyed, bushy-tailed and eager to please. The way the jazz teacher, Mrs Merman, always said, "Smile, children, smile," made Olivia want to snarl with rage and bite her.

Katie finished and everyone clapped politely. Sebastian Shaw made a few remarks, suggesting that sometimes in acting less could be more, and then looked around the class.

"Now, what do other people think?" Everyone hesitated. Nobody wanted to speak first. Mr Shaw's eye lit on Olivia sitting under her curtain of hair.

"Olivia, do you have an opinion?"

Olivia turned very pink and said nothing. She wished she could disappear. Everyone was looking at her.

"Olivia?" repeated Sebastian Shaw firmly.

Olivia looked up from under her hair at the expectant faces. She thought she heard somebody giggle and whisper, "It watches, but does it talk?" The words rose angrily in her throat, very loudly and clearly: "It's silly. I think acting is silly. What's the point of pretending to be other people when you can just be yourself? It's just lying by another name. And there's no real risk; it's not like when you see someone doing something really dangerous such as flying through the air on a trapeze and having to grasp someone else's hand mid-air or hurtling head first down a pole. That's real, and the consequences of getting it wrong are real too. If you don't catch the hand or you don't stop in time at the bottom of the pole, you'll get injured very badly or die. But nobody in a play really dies. Acting is just faking it."

A murmur of surprise passed around the class, and Katie flushed scarlet. Some people started to protest at what Olivia had said, but Mr Shaw raised a hand to silence them.

"I think what Olivia has said is very interesting. Olivia, have you ever seen a play?" asked Mr Shaw gently.

Olivia shook her head fiercely. "I don't want to either." Her eyes flashed dangerously.

"Well, I hope that I will eventually

persuade you to change your mind, Olivia, because sometimes a play, a good play, tells more truths in two hours than most people discover in a lifetime. It allows us to experience things and feel emotions, sometimes terrible things and emotions, in a way so powerful that it becomes unnecessary for us to feel or perform those things ourselves in real life. Great acting isn't about lying, it's about daring to be totally honest. Great acting wears no clothes, it is completely naked.

"Olivia, I once saw your father on the high-wire crossing between two skyscrapers in New York; it was thrilling and felt as if I was watching something very dangerous. But I also saw your mother play Rosalind in *As You Like It* here in London and that was thrilling, and I felt as if I was watching something very dangerous then too. In both cases the performer was utterly fearless. They gave themselves completely."

He spoke with such passion that the entire class was silenced, and the quiet was broken only by the sound of the bell going for the next lesson. Mr Shaw had to rush off and everyone began to collect their belongings.

Olivia stood up and walked towards the

door, acutely aware that everyone was watching her.

"The cheek of it! Her, somebody so completely talentless, lecturing *us* on acting," said Katie loudly and scornfully.

"I don't think she meant it like that," said Georgia quietly.

"Oh yes, she did, dummy. And she said I was silly," said Katie.

"No, she didn't," said Aeysha soothingly. "She said that *acting* was silly. I don't think she's right but it's a point of view. I mean, I find football boring but loads of people think it's ace."

"Either way," said Katie ominously. "From now on, Olivia Marvell is dead."

Chapter Fifteen

Abbie Cardew had taken Olivia up to a small rehearsal room right at the top of the school. She was trying to help Olivia do a *grand plié.*

"That's much better, you've almost got it right," said Abbie encouragingly, although in truth what Olivia was doing was a very long way from right. It was, thought Abbie patiently, a bit like trying to teach a newborn foal to dance. Olivia had the best sense of balance that Abbie had ever encountered – she could tumble, do cartwheels and back flips like a professional acrobat – but she seemed incapable of grasping the technique of any dance form, whether it was ballet, tap or contemporary. She was all gangly arms and legs. Privately Abbie suspected it wasn't that Olivia couldn't dance but that she *wouldn't* dance; unlike her little sister, she just didn't want to. But Miss Swan had asked her to try and help Olivia, and Abbie was going to do her best. Besides, she liked the younger girl with her dark soulful eyes and serious face, and although Olivia never complained, Abbie knew that she wasn't happy.

The last three weeks had been the worst of Olivia's life. Eel had taken to the Swan like a cygnet to water. She was in seventh heaven. She loved the routine, the morning academic lessons followed by long afternoons of dancing, singing and acting, rushing between classes and discovering the amazing things that her body could do. Once upon a time, all her teachers had despaired of her, but now she was considered a star in the making and encouraged to take as many dance classes as possible. Whereas Olivia, who had always been such a rising star in the circus, was just a nobody.

Sometimes Eel's enthusiasm for the Swan made Olivia feel furious. Only yesterday evening Olivia had become so infuriated by Eel watching herself perform for hours in front of the mirror in their shared bedroom that she had called Eel a "stage-school brat".

"No, I'm not," said Eel reasonably. "I just want to be very good at dancing, and you can't get good at anything unless you practise for hours and hours. Gran says it doesn't matter how talented you are, if you don't put in the work you'll never be really brilliant. And I want to be the bestest dancer in the Swan, in the country and in the entire universe."

"Oh," said Olivia nastily, "so little Miss Twinkletoes wants to shine, does she? Just like Katie Wilkes-Cox."

Eel had looked hurt and replied, "I'm just getting the chance to do something I really like, and do it well. You should be pleased for me, but you're being really horrid, Olivia, and behaving like a boar with a sore head."

"Bear," snapped Olivia. Eel had stomped away.

Olivia knew she was behaving badly, but she couldn't stop herself being sulky and sullen. Every day was a trial. Because of their complete lack of experience, both Olivia and Eel had been put in the dance classes with the youngest children who had only just joined the school in Year Three. It was all right for Eel, who showed every sign that she would soon surpass them.

Her obvious talent and sunny nature had already made Eel popular with the other children, and she'd quickly made friends. But Olivia, who was tall for her age, continued to feel like a clumsy giant among all the smaller children, and was acutely aware of Katie Wilkes-Cox and the little gang around her. Whenever Katie passed her in the corridor, she would come as close as she could and whisper, "Baby ballet," and then fall about laughing as if she had said something supremely witty.

"Olivia, I've got to go. Miss Swan promised to run through my song with me," said Abbie, who was through to the final round of auditions to play Liesl in a new West End production of *The Sound of Music*. She glanced at her watch. "There's ten minutes before the bell for afternoon lessons; why don't you go through what we've just practised and we'll meet here tomorrow at the same time." Abbie picked up her things and rushed off, humming, "You are Sixteen Going on Seventeen" under her breath.

Olivia sighed and wandered over to the big open windows. She looked across the rooftops of London. In the distance she could see Tower Bridge. Her attention was caught by a large bird swooping on to the flat roof of the building next door. The building, which was derelict, had a low parapet around the roof with large iron spikes sticking out, and it was just below here on a sheltered ledge that the bird had nested. Olivia could see the edge of the nest. The bird hopped on the parapet, eyeing Olivia inquisitively across the five metres that separated the two high buildings. Olivia rummaged in her bag, found a half-eaten sandwich that she had bought from the school cafeteria and crumbled it on to the window ledge of the rehearsal room. The bird watched her closely, but didn't come any nearer.

"You're like me, little bird, you're scared," whispered Olivia softly. The bird tilted its head as if listening to her. "But you are freer than me; at least you can fly away. I'm stuck here doing silly ballet and stupid tap until Dad comes back for us. I can't even practise my tightrope-walking, and that's the only thing that makes me forget myself." Thinking of her dad and what stunt he might be planning made Olivia feel anxious. A tear ran down her cheek.

She crumbled the last of the sandwich on to the window ledge in the hope the bird might come and peck at it, and turned back to the rehearsal room. She sighed and decided to practise as Abbie had suggested.

She held on to the barre and made a few awkward movements. Immediately she was aware of stifled giggles behind her, and whirled round. Katie Wilkes-Cox, Kylie Morris, Georgia Jones and some other girls were standing in front of the plate-glass observation window. Abbie had forgotten to pull the blind down so that nobody could see in. Katie was imitating Olivia's ungainly movements in a manner that was very cruel but also very funny. Georgia and Aeysha looked embarrassed but the others were doubled over laughing, and Katie said loudly, "Some Swan! More like an ugly duckling!"

Peals of laughter followed the girls as they ran down the corridor. Olivia stood numbly in the rehearsal room until the sound died away and the bell went for afternoon practice.

Chapter Sixteen

Georgia was playing the piano in one of the music practice rooms. She didn't really want to practise, even though she had her grade-three exam coming up at Christmas, but she didn't want to be on her own, either. Since the day of the newbies' concert, Katie had been particularly snide and unpleasant to Georgia, as if she was testing her loyalty.

"Oh, look, here comes Miss Clumsy Clots!" she'd say every time Georgia came near, and she excluded Georgia from a sleepover party. Aeysha had been really apologetic about going, but Georgia didn't blame her; if it had been the other way round she'd have probably gone too. When the Queen Bee called, they all buzzed.

Georgia finished playing her piece and

sighed. She couldn't keep away from Katie; she wanted her approval and she wanted to be invited to the swimming-pool party that she had heard was being planned, but she hated herself for it. She felt like a puppet on a string. She wanted to break free of the puppet master but she couldn't bear the thought of being alone at a time when home was so sad and miserable. Only that morning, her mum had said that she was going to have to make an appointment to see Miss Swan.

"I promise that I'll do anything I can to keep you at the Swan, Georgia. But I can't promise the impossible. I want you to know that I really am trying my best." Georgia had pushed aside her cereal bowl and given her mum a big hug, but her stomach had lurched at the thought that she might have to leave.

She started playing a Mozart piece. She wasn't playing well but Olivia, walking past the room, heard the music and was transported back to a glorious summer in Ireland when Jack had used the same piece for part of his act. Quietly she opened the door and crept in to listen.

"I enjoyed your playing," she said when Georgia had finished.

Georgia turned round and smiled hesitantly. "I like it because it sounds how I feel inside."

"Sad?" said Olivia, surprised.

Georgia nodded.

"But you always look pretty happy to me."

"It's called putting an act," said Georgia. She took a deep breath. "Sometimes I think I'm better at *acting* being me than I am at actually *being* me." She beckoned Olivia over to squeeze next to her on the piano stool and they sat together, their backs to the open door.

"Sometimes," said Olivia, "I don't like being me at all and wish I could be someone else. I used to be comfortable in my own skin. I knew who I was, what I was good at and where I belonged in the universe. Now I don't even recognise myself. I'm snappy and miserable all the time. How do you bear it here?"

Georgia looked surprised. "But I love it at the Swan! I'm dead scared that I'm going to have to leave. My mum doesn't think she can manage the fees after the end of this term. I love the singing and the dancing and the acting. I know you think acting is silly, but when you're doing it, it doesn't feel silly at all – it's thrilling – and when you're doing it well you can feel that the audience is thrilled too. They believe entirely in the world that you are creating; for that moment nothing else matters to them or to you. It's as if your entire life, your past and your future only exists in that single moment."

"I feel like that when I'm on the wire," said Olivia.

"The wire?" asked Georgia.

"The high-wire."

"You can do that?" Georgia asked admiringly.

"Yup."

"That's so cool. Can I watch you?" asked Georgia shyly.

"Fat chance," replied Olivia grumpily. "My gran hates the circus and there's nowhere to practise."

"Bet you're amazing."

"Really?" said Olivia with sarcasm in her voice. "I'm the baby ballet girl, remember. The one you and your friend Katie Wilkes-Cox make fun of at every chance."

Georgia turned beetroot red. "I never meant—" she protested.

"But you still do it," snapped Olivia. There

was an uncomfortable silence.

"I know it's no excuse, but I don't join in."

"But you're there, and you don't say anything and you never raise a finger to stop it, do you? I don't know if that makes you any better than Katie, and in fact it might make you worse. You let somebody else do the dirty work, look anguished but you don't actually protest."

"No," whispered Georgia. "I don't. I'm a coward."

Olivia looked at her. "Oh, please don't cry, Georgia," said Olivia. "I'm as much a coward as you are. I never tell anyone what she's doing. But I've made such a bad start at the Swan, I know that nobody would believe me. She may be a rubbish Miranda, but Katie's a very good little actress. In front of the teachers she acts as if butter wouldn't melt in her mouth. She opens her eyes wide and smiles that irritating little smile and everybody falls for it, even my gran."

She looked hard at Georgia. "Even you aren't prepared to speak up against her when she's done something truly dreadful. You didn't fall at the newbies' concert, did you? You were pushed, and you think Katie did it."

Georgia gasped. "How do you know that?"

"You don't have to be Sherlock Holmes to work it out. I saw you come through that curtain like a rocket and I saw who benefited because you couldn't go on. But, of course, as long as you protest that it was an accident, nobody's going to think differently and Katie's in the clear."

"You won't blab, will you, Olivia?" said Georgia, looking panic-stricken.

"Of course I won't. I'm a coward, remember, just like you. Anyway, nobody would believe me; they all think I'm some kind of freak. But then I think Katie's a monster."

"Her dad's awful. If I had a dad like that, I'd just want to curl up and die," said Georgia.

"Yes, we saw him," said Olivia. She mimicked Mr Wilkes-Cox. "Katie, you're a little star! What have you got to do, Katie? You've got to shine, Katie, shine!"

"Shine, Katie, shine!" repeated Georgia, exaggerating the words to comic effect. Olivia and Georgia burst out laughing and they didn't notice Katie standing listening at the open door. She had a face like thunder and she was clenching her fists.

Olivia suddenly stopped laughing. "We're being as bad as she is," she said guiltily.

"Totally," said Georgia seriously. "We are. But at least Katie will never know what we said."

Chapter Seventeen

After her conversation with Georgia, Olivia put some effort into finding somewhere she could walk the wire. But she had no luck and she soon lost heart. Most rehearsal spaces in the school were in constant use all day, and even after school and at weekends they were in demand for extra classes and practice sessions.

Space was cramped at the Swan and it wasn't unusual to find someone practising their cello at the bottom of the stairs or even learning lines in a broom cupboard. Olivia had once come across a line of girls tap-dancing in the toilets and an older boy doing one of Hamlet's soliloquies when she had gone to get something from the stationery cupboard. In desperation, Olivia had gone to the park and rigged her wire between the branches of two trees, but a small crowd had gathered, which she found unnerving, and eventually a park-keeper had arrived and told her grumpily that it was against by-law 426, subsection 212 to tightrope-walk in the park.

It was Georgia who had thought of the rehearsal room at the top of the school, and she had told Eel during their contemporary dance class one afternoon. Immediately after school Eel marched Olivia up the stairs and pointed out the hook by the mirror on the wall next to the door.

She wanted to do something to shake her sister out of her misery. Olivia had taken to walking around with a pained look on her face, as if she had just received a particularly tragic piece of news. Eel hated to see Olivia so unhappy, but she didn't know what she could do about it, she was so busy discovering new friends and new skills. Besides, the routine at the Swan was so punishing that by the time she crawled up the stairs to the flat some evenings, she could barely keep her eyes open. Trying to have a heart-to-heart with Olivia just felt more than she could cope with, particularly when Olivia was so snappy all the time.

Only last night there had been another scene. After supper, Alicia had said, "Now then, Eel, would you like to look at this ballet book with me and I'll read you the story of *Swan Lake*?" Eel didn't hesitate. Straight away she clambered on to Alicia's lap and snuggled down with her thumb in her mouth. Olivia said nothing, but inside she was screaming, "Traitor!"

Alicia saw Olivia's forlorn face. "Why don't you join us?" she said, patting the sofa beside her.

Olivia shook her head. "I hate ballet," she said, scowling. She got up and went into her bedroom, slamming the door behind her.

Alicia raised an eyebrow but said nothing. She'd waited a while before poking her head around the door, but Olivia pretended to be asleep.

Olivia had lain in bed listening to her gran and Eel laughing, and a tear of self-pity slid down her cheek. It was so unfair. She had tried to look after Eel as much as she could since their mother had died and now when she needed a bit of looking-after, Eel had abandoned her.

"Livy, are you listening? This room's perfect!"

exclaimed Eel, bouncing up and down with excitement. "Georgia says it's almost always free after school or at weekends because it's too small for anything other than voice classes or one-to-ones. You can use that hook for one end of the wire, and there's even a dusty old cupboard that no one ever opens where you can leave your suitcase. And nobody can see in if you remember to pull the blind down."

"The hook's fine, but what about the other end?" asked Olivia tonelessly.

"There!" said Eel, executing a perfect *jeté* towards the window and pointing to one of the iron spikes on the derelict building next door. Eel beamed. She felt very grown up, helping her big sister.

Olivia looked at the spike through narrowed eyes. "It'll never work," she said doubtfully.

"It won't if you don't try it," said Eel impatiently. "What's happened to you, Livy? You say that the only thing that would make your time here at the Swan bearable is if you can practise on the high-wire, but when I show how you can, you just make excuses." Then she added fiercely, "I wouldn't ever let anything stop me dancing. I'd rather die."

"Maybe I've lost my nerve, just like Dad," said Olivia miserably.

"No, you haven't, you're just feeling sorry for yourself," returned Eel, looking at her big sister. She saw Olivia's eyes fill with tears.

"I'm so worried about him, Eel. I'm sure he's planning some big stunt, and I know he hasn't got the confidence to pull it off. It could make him do something reckless. But every time I try to talk to him about it when he rings, he changes the subject."

"The Great Marvello, the world's most fearless tightrope-walker, would never do anything stupid," said Eel confidently.

"No, Eel, you're right. The Great Marvello wouldn't take a stupid risk, but Jack Marvell, penniless single father of two, might. I think he's pretty desperate for us all to be together again, and desperate to prove to Alicia and to himself that he can do it." Olivia sighed. "If only I could think of a way of making some money."

"Well, when I'm the world's most famous dancer, I'll have lots of money," said Eel, clowning around to distract her sister. "But you'll have to wait until I'm grown up, then I'll give you all my spare millions." She smiled, pleased with her own generosity. "Come on. Let's see if that spike will hold."

"I'm too tired, Eel," said Olivia. "All that silly prancing around all day is knackering."

But Eel wasn't listening. She picked up one end of the wire and attached it to the hook. Then, holding the other end, she leaned out of the window and aimed for the spike on the building next door. She had to have a couple of goes, but at last she succeeded and clapped her own prowess. Then she moved a chair close to the wire, jumped up and wobbled along it like a jelly in a high wind.

"See?" she said. "I'm right. It's completely perfect." She leapt down and curtsied to an unseen audience. Olivia walked slowly over to the wire and jumped on. She took several steps forwards and then several backwards. She did a flip, and as she straightened up again, Eel could see Olivia's eyes shining as if she had been brought back to life after a long, long sleep, like Sleeping Beauty.

"Eel, thank you, you're a genius."

"I know," said Eel smugly, and she did a little twirl.

Chapter Eighteen

An Indian summer had arrived in London. It was surprisingly hot for so late in the year. In the top rehearsal room Olivia was perched on the wire, watched by Eel, who every now and again exploded into pirouettes, whirling around the room like a dervish and admiring her reflection in the mirrors. The windows were wide open to let what little air there was into the space. The bird from the nest was sitting on the rehearsal-room window sill, pecking at the remains of a biscuit. It was becoming tamer and tamer by the day, often appearing on the verge of flying right into the room. Olivia's face was flushed with triumph as she walked across the wire. It felt good to be back on the tightrope; it was where she had always felt most at home.

Olivia spent every spare moment secretly practising her tightrope-walking, and although she was still unhappy and anxious about their father, when she was on the wire her misery and worry receded to a distant dull ache. Sometimes she forgot about everything and leapt along the wire as if she was flying like a bird. Even her dancing improved a little, although she was still in the lowest classes for all her dance lessons, quite alone now among the younger children because Eel had already moved up two grades.

Olivia finished doing a tumble on the tightrope. Eel clapped appreciatively. She looked at the clock.

"I've got a private dance lesson. Can you get the wire off the spike on your own?" This required real patience to ease it off each time.

"No problem, I seem to have got the knack at last. You go, I want to practise a little more," said Olivia.

Eel slipped away and Olivia got back on the wire, soon lost in the effort of trying to do a particularly difficult manoeuvre that involved walking on her hands. Several times she slipped, but at last she succeeded. She jumped down from the wire, elated.

She was startled by the sound of clapping and spun round, realising that she'd again forgotten to close the blinds on the observation glass. There had been a few times during the last week when she'd had the feeling that somebody was watching her, and she'd worried that it was Katie and her gang. But it couldn't be Katie today, because everyone knew she was having a swimming-pool party. Olivia looked round and was confronted by a shock of red hair and the wide smile of Tom McCavity, who opened the door and sauntered in.

"Have you been spying on me?" asked Olivia furiously. "I suppose you came to have a laugh. Everybody else does, so why shouldn't you join in the fun too?"

"Whoa!" said Tom, backing away with his hands raised. "You really are very fierce, Olivia Marvell. I think you probably take after your gran more than you realise." He grinned. "Actually, I just came to get my homework diary. I left it here after voice class yesterday, and I'm very glad I did. You're a bit of a dark horse. That was some display of tightrope-walking. It was awesome!"

"You're not teasing me?" said Olivia

uncertainly, her voice full of suspicion. Tom shook his head vigorously.

"Katie Wilkes-Cox said you had been in some kind of travelling freak show, but Katie's a snobby little cow. I knew from Mr Shaw that your dad is a high-wire walker and somebody else said you'd been in a circus too, but quite honestly I doubted that. I've seen you dancing, and I didn't believe that anyone who could trip over their own feet quite so often as you do could possibly be in a circus, unless perhaps they were a clown, and you always look far too serious for that." Olivia opened her mouth indignantly, but Tom put up a hand to silence her. "But, hey, clearly I was wrong." He beamed, and it was as if the room was full of light. "You're brilliant. Completely amazing. Do you think you could teach me?"

"Well, I could try," said Olivia shyly, surprising herself.

"Right," said Tom. "There's no time like the present. Let's get started."

"OK," said Olivia, getting carried along by his enthusiasm. "But it's our secret. My gran must never find out. She hates anything to do with the circus."

"Oh," said Tom, "so you're not her spy, then?"

Olivia burst out laughing. "Wherever did you get that idea? It's ludicrous. We hardly talk. I think she hates me because I don't have a talent like Eel."

"Oh, but you do," said Tom. "Everyone can dance to a greater or lesser degree. But very few people can walk the high-wire, and you're one of them. I'm dead impressed."

Chapter Nineteen

A few miles away, Georgia was lazing beside Katie's swimming pool, sipping a sparkling peach juice. The smell of barbecuing chicken wafted across the garden. She and some of the other girls in the class had been invited to spend the day at the Wilkes-Cox home.

"Only the select few, the people who really count," said Katie loudly, as she handed out the invites at the end of maths on Friday morning.

"Oh, so not the people who actually *can* count," said Tom, with a wicked smile.

Katie blushed and looked annoyed. She had hoped that nobody had noticed that she'd come bottom of the class again in a maths test. Maintaining good standards in schoolwork was part of the deal at the Swan. Pupils who fell behind in their academic classes were barred from attending auditions for professional work and couldn't participate in the many concerts and performances that the school put on until they'd caught up.

Katie had set her heart on being part of the Swan team this year for the Children's Royal Spectacular, particularly as it meant appearing on TV. She wasn't going to let an inability to grasp basic algebra stand in the way of stardom. Her dad had said that algebra didn't matter and he was quite sure that Miss Swan must make exceptions for really talented pupils. She barged past Tom to give Georgia her invitation.

"For my special and loyal friend, Georgia," said Katie, pointedly. Georgia felt as if Katie's words were more of a threat than a compliment, and a look of uncertainty crossed her face. Katie grabbed her hard by the wrist, and hissed, "No excuses, Georgia," so intimidatingly that Georgia felt almost frightened.

Now, as she sat by the swimming pool listening to the other girls chatting all around her, she realised that she felt intensely lonely. Katie's sly behaviour towards Olivia was making her feel more and more uncomfortable.

Georgia felt sorry for Olivia and admired the way she never answered back to any of the taunts. After her encounter with Olivia in the practice room, she had suggested to Katie that they stop picking on her, but Katie had looked at Georgia as if she was something the cat had brought in and said, "Please yourself, but don't expect me to be your friend. You only want to suck up to her because she's old Swan's granddaughter. Unfortunately, she's the talentless one. That Eel girl may be worth making a friend of, although I sincerely doubt she's half as gifted as people say she is, but Liver Duckface Swan is a total waste of space. She can't dance, she can't sing. She can't do anything. I reckon when old Swan eventually twigs quite how useless she is, she'll pack her off to school somewhere else. She won't want her holding back the children with real star potential like us."

Georgia was so thrilled by Katie's "like us" that she let the matter drop. She knew that she was a coward for going along with Katie and, even though she tried to play as small a part as possible in tormenting Olivia, she felt guilty every time they were in a room together. Once or twice she had given Olivia a rueful little smile, not at all surprised to get back only a stony stare.

Chapter Twenty

Georgia trailed her fingers in the pool and tuned back in to what the other girls were saying.

"We're going to Egypt for Christmas," said Aeysha.

"Oh, I've been there," said Katie. "It was boring. Just sand and history. It's the pits."

"I think the pyramids are interesting—" started Georgia, seeing Aeysha's face drop, but Katie talked over her.

"We're going to Dubai," said Katie. "It's going to be awesome. My dad's got business there. It's supposed to be fantastic. The height of luxury. It's got the tallest building in the world. Totally." She turned to Georgia. "So what thrilling things have you got planned, little Miss Georgia Jones?"

The tone was sweet but Georgia knew the question was treacherous. She squirmed. She wouldn't be going anywhere. The best she could hope for was that her mum might manage a few days off work and that they would go to some museums together. Her favourite was the V&A because sometimes there were exhibitions of costumes and intricate miniature designs for stage sets. Georgia enjoyed these days out with her mum, riding on the top deck of the bus together and eating her mum's special cheese and Marmite doorstep sandwiches and home-made brownies. They laughed a lot together, and it always reminded Georgia of a time when her mother hadn't looked so tired and worried.

She opened her mouth to say, "Nothing much," but then she glimpsed a strange expression on Katie's face. It was almost triumphant, as if she was really enjoying making Georgia feel small, and poor, and bad about herself. Suddenly Georgia found herself saying, "Actually, my mum's taking me to New York. We're flying first class and staying in a five-star hotel."

"Wicked!" said Aeysha. "You *are* lucky. That easily tops Egypt and Dubai."

Georgia felt a feeling of warmth seep through her. It was nice being the interesting and glamorous one for a change, the centre of attention, not just someone always on the edge of things.

"Yes, that's the best," agreed the others enviously; all except Katie, who looked at Georgia through narrowed eyes. "I thought your mum didn't have any money," she said.

"Wherever did you get that idea, Katie?" said Georgia. "She's loaded. We just don't like to talk about. My mum thinks it's vulgar to talk about money and splash out on big houses and cars."

It was the most effective piece of acting that Georgia had done in her entire life. She was saved from further explanation by Katie's dad announcing that the barbecue was ready and inviting everyone to load their plates with chicken and burgers, and help themselves to baked potatoes, corn on the cob and bowls of coleslaw. Georgia made sure she sat as far away from Katie as possible, but every time she looked up she saw Katie staring at her, smiling her dangerous, cat-like smile, and she felt worried.

Georgia knew she ought to confess that of

course she wasn't going to New York, explain that she had only been joking and that she and her mum were poorer than the average church mouse – she couldn't even afford new jazz shoes, for heaven's sake! But Aeysha was saying how envious she was of Georgia going to the Big Apple, how she had always dreamed of going there, and Georgia knew with a sinking feeling that if she admitted she'd lied now, she would look like a complete idiot. What's more, Katie would never let her forget it and would take great pleasure in telling the whole school that Georgia Jones was a liar and a fantasist.

So instead she found herself unhappily embroidering the lie, telling Aeysha that she and her mum planned to see a Broadway show and go shopping on Fifth Avenue. In fact she was almost beginning to believe it herself when Katie said brightly, "Well, Georgia, as you're so rich, you'll have to promise to bring us all back presents, won't she, girls?"

Everyone murmured their approval at this plan, and Georgia found herself turning red and muttering, "I'll see what I can do." She pushed aside the rest of her chicken. Suddenly she didn't feel hungry any more.

After lunch they swam again, but all the pleasure had evaporated for Georgia and she kept wondering how long it would be before Aeysha's dad came to pick them up. He was giving her a lift home because her mum was working, even though it was a Saturday.

Then Katie showed them her mum's room, and opened the massive cupboards so they could try on some of her designer clothes and shoes. They were all giggling and clomping around in heels far too big and high for them when Katie suddenly produced a key and unlocked a jewellery box on the dressing table. She casually pulled out a glittering necklace, studded with hundreds of diamonds and emeralds, and posed with it around her neck.

"It's worth thousands," she boasted.

"Won't your mum be angry with us for playing with it?" said Aeysha, looking worried.

"Of course not," said Katie scornfully. "We're not going to lose it, and even if we did, she could just buy another one."

She looked at Georgia. "I expect your mum's got loads of jewels, hasn't she, Georgia?"

Georgia felt flustered. "Er, totally, of course she has. Masses."

"What kind?" enquired Katie.

"Oh, you know, diamonds, rubies," said Georgia, waving her arm and trying to think of other precious stones. She suddenly remembered her mum's Victorian garnet and topaz ring. Her mum had said that it wasn't worth very much, but it was very pretty and unusual and she cherished it because it reminded her of somebody she loved and that made it unique, worth more than all the money in the world.

"Actually, she has a ring that's priceless because it's so incredibly rare. It's the only one of its kind in the world. It's an old family heirloom," said Georgia.

"Oh," said Katie dangerously. "We'd like to see that, wouldn't we, girls?" The others nodded, and even before Katie opened her mouth again, Georgia felt her stomach plummeting like an out-of-control lift.

"You'd better bring it into school for us all to see, little Miss Jones. Otherwise we might not believe you. We might think that you're telling porky pies, not just about the ring but about other things too."

Again, it was sweetly said, but the threat was unmistakable, and Georgia knew it was now or never to come clean and admit that New York was only a fantasy. But at that moment Katie's dad called upstairs to say Aeysha's father had arrived and it was time to go home.

Chapter Twenty-One

Miss Swan gazed out at the Swan pupils, her sharp eyes passing over the faces of the children. They were all gathered in the theatre for assembly. Everyone loved these assemblies because it was a chance to hear about upcoming auditions, and to find out who had got bookings and in which shows and movies. Last week Alicia announced that all three main roles in the remake of *The Railway Children* had gone to Swan pupils, and that the latest release by a former pupil, the singer-songwriter Amber Lavelle, who had only left the school three years ago, had gone straight to number one.

Alicia was pleased to see Eel clowning around with her friends. The child was a real character and had settled down well at the school, already fulfilling the promise that Alicia had spotted. She was doing well academically, and she was affectionate too, often curling up on Alicia's lap in the evenings.

Alicia's eye fell on Olivia, standing close to the rest of her form and yet somehow completely detached from them. As ever, Olivia looked as if she was weighed down by some terrible burden. Alicia wished she knew how to help her granddaughter, who was clearly unhappy. But every approach that she made, every attempt to get Olivia to open up, was politely rebuffed.

Alicia felt that she was somehow failing Olivia, but she didn't know what to do to put it right, and if Olivia wouldn't let her near, she knew she never *would* know. The child would always remain a stranger to her. Olivia had suddenly taken to disappearing for long periods and when Alicia asked her where she was spending her time, she clammed up so decisively it made Alicia feel like a thief trying to steal a pearl from an oyster.

Her gaze moved on across the auditorium. Tom McCavity and William Todd were making their classmates laugh. One who wasn't laughing was Georgia Jones, who was looking pinched and almost as unhappy as Olivia. Alicia knew from a tiny comment made by Mrs Jones when she had come to pick Georgia up from the newbies' concert that money was tight at the moment and she wondered whether she should offer a scholarship. She didn't want to lose Georgia, who had real talent and who could be a great asset to the Swan, perhaps even one of its stars. She decided she would invite Georgia's mum in for a chat.

Her gaze fell on Katie Wilkes-Cox, who was eyeing Tom and William disdainfully, and Alicia sighed. That child was spoiled rotten by her dreadful parents and she was often rude to teachers and dismissive of the achievements of other children. Her schoolwork was getting worse too.

Alicia knew she would have to do something about Katie before things got out of hand. When she accepted a child at the Swan, she felt that she was making a commitment to that child and she would do anything to avoid breaking it. But Alicia wondered whether Katie might turn out to be one of her few failures. Katie's talent wasn't in question, but her attitude certainly was. If there was one thing

Alicia wouldn't stand at the school, it was prima donnas who thought themselves a cut above everyone else.

Alicia raised a hand and the children fell silent.

"A good morning to you all. Now, I have two very important announcements to make. There is good news and there is some bad news. I'll give you the bad news first. This is very serious, I'm afraid, very serious. I fear we have a thief in our midst."

A murmur rippled through the room.

"Money and valuable items have gone missing from the rehearsal room at the top of the school. Miss Hanbury's gold chain broke while she was giving a voice class in there the day before yesterday. She left it on the window ledge and forgot all about it. When she returned a few hours later, it had gone, and it hasn't been handed in. She is very upset because it was a gift from her fiancé. Several pupils have also reported money and jewellery disappearing from that particular room. Aeysha, you lost a bracelet, didn't you, dear?"

Aeysha nodded.

"I would urge you to take care of your

possessions and not to bring anything valuable into school." Alicia paused and gazed at the faces in the room. Several people blushed and everybody, even the most innocent, felt a little bit guilty inside. "If anybody has any information that they would like to share in confidence, or indeed any items that they would like to hand over, then please do feel free to come and see me in my study. Nobody should be afraid. Whoever is responsible for the thefts needs help, not punishment. They will be treated fairly. Whoever you are, we can sort this out, but you must return all the missing items."

Alicia paused again.

"Now to the good news! Tomorrow we will be holding auditions to select those who will be part of this year's Swan entry for the Children's Royal Spectacular at the London Palladium. I'd like as many of you as possible to give it your best shot. Even if you don't make the grade, the audition experience will be good for you, particularly for those of you who might be put forward for the *Sound of Music* auditions just before Christmas. Besides, we want the very best people. The Swan does not just have some of the most talented children in the country, it has the best trained, so we want to show the whole world what we can do. It's a terrific showcase for you and the school. We want to make sure that the Swan wins through the TV heats and is top of the bill!"

A huge cheer erupted in the theatre.

Chapter Twenty-Two

Eel took a deep breath as the music started. Immediately she was totally immersed in the dance. It was as if there was nothing else in the world except her and her body. There was a fire in the place where her heart was, and her limbs felt as if they had become molten, allowing her to do the impossible. She felt both exhilarated and incredibly calm too, as if nothing else in the world mattered except the dance. She felt as if she was flying, not dancing. She soared as the music reached its climax and turned a final sequence of explosive cartwheels, coming to a standstill on stage with a little flourish.

Eel beamed from ear to ear, still feeling as if she was floating two metres above the ground. But had she done enough to persuade Granny

Alicia to include her in the Swan team for the Children's Royal Spectacular? Eel hoped so, but she knew it was an outside chance. Almost everyone at the Swan had more experience and more training than her. She was pretty well a complete beginner as a dancer, and while she had bucketfuls of natural ability, that would count for very little against the impressive technique of many of the other pupils. Sometimes Eel and her friends went to watch the seniors practise and Eel hoped that one day she would be as good as some of them. She thought Abbie Cardew was wonderful, practically perfect in every way.

"Thank you very much, Eel. Results will be posted on the board at the end of the week." Eel curtsied, said, "Thank you," and left. *Please, please, let me be in it,* she thought, giving the audition panel her cheekiest grin.

Alicia smiled and watched her go.

"Of course, we can't possibly include her," she murmured to her fellow judges. "She's only been here a few weeks."

"Why not?" replied India Taylor. "She may only be seven but she's got more self-possession than the average seventeen-year-old. She's much more confident than her sister. I think it might be good for her. And she's working like a Trojan. Performing before a live audience might be just the thing to spur her on to greater heights. A dangling carrot, as it were."

"I think she developed a taste for live performance at the newbies' concert," said Alicia wryly. "But maybe you're right. At the very least, she'd charm the judges and the audience into voting for the Swan, and we might need all the help we can get. I'll put her on the Possible list." She looked at her sheet. "Who's next? Ah, Georgia Jones, how nice."

Georgia walked nervously on to the stage and stood in the spotlight.

"When you're ready, Georgia," said Alicia.

Georgia wasn't sure she would be truly ready ever again. This was the first time she had performed properly since the catastrophe of the newbies' concert. She felt sick inside in case she made a fool of herself. She had started to doubt her abilities more and more. Maybe Katie was right; maybe she was just a clumsy oaf.

Alicia peered at Georgia. "Are you all right, dear?" she asked, a look of concern on her face.

Georgia nodded, but she didn't feel it. Mrs Collett at the piano began to play. Georgia opened her mouth but nothing came out.

"Begin again, dear," said Alicia. Once again, Mrs Collett played the intro and Georgia opened her mouth a second time. Then she burst into tears and rushed off stage, where she was sick into the fire bucket in the wings.

She knew that she had blown it. There would be no Children's Royal Spectacular for her. She felt defeated, as if all the long years of hard practice had been for nothing. It didn't matter if her mum couldn't pay the fees because Miss Swan would probably ask her to leave anyway. Georgia knew she had performed badly in almost every lesson since the newbies' concert; most of her teachers had expressed disappointment in her. Georgia felt a total failure.

Katie breezed through the wings with Kylie Morris in tow. "Oh, yuk, Georgia Jones, that's gross!" she cried. "Get a grip, can't you, you'll put the rest of us off. My dad always says that if you can't stand the heat, stay out of the kitchen. Losers like you shouldn't even *try* to compete with people of genuine talent."

Back in the auditorium, Alicia asked Abbie to go and check that Georgia was all right, then she turned to the rest of the panel. "I wish I knew what was worrying that child. It's as if her accident has knocked every shred of confidence out of her. She hasn't been the same since the newbies' concert."

"Shall I put her on the No list?" asked Miss Hanbury.

"If you all don't mind, I'd like to suggest a private audition in my office. If I can be sure she's up to it, being included in the team might be just the boost she needs."

The others nodded.

"Next!" called Alicia.

Katie walked on stage, tossing her hair, and with great aplomb launched into "Truly Scrumptious" from *Chitty Chitty Bang Bang*. Her routine included a highly polished tap-dancing interlude. Katie felt invincible. She knew she was making a good impression. A place in the team was hers for sure. She curtsied and walked off, humming "Popular" under her breath.

"A bit too sweet for me," said Sebastian.

"Yes," agreed Alicia, "but not a performance you can really fault."

"She's good, even if she's not quite as good as she thinks she is," said Miss Taylor.

"I agree," said Miss Hanbury. "I'm not sure we can afford to leave her out. She's very strong."

"Not in maths she isn't," said Alicia ominously. She looked at her watch. "I think Katie was the last one. I'm going to find Georgia and see if I can persuade her to perform for me, and then we'll reconvene at teatime to try and finalise the team."

Chapter Twenty-Three

Katie sat on a chair in Miss Swan's study. She had put on her most serious expression and appeared to be listening intently to every word that Alicia was saying. Alicia was studying some papers in her hand and she looked stern.

"You do realise that this is all very unsatisfactory, don't you, Katie? You have failed to hand in your last three maths assignments, and your results in class are poor. According to your form tutor, your performance in English and science is not much better. What do you have to say?"

"I'm very sorry, Miss Swan, I really am," said Katie, opening her eyes wide because her dad said it made her look like an adorable kitten. "I know I've been underperforming in lessons, but I've been trying so hard to concentrate on my dance. Miss Taylor says that I'm improving very fast. Yesterday she said I was one of the best in school."

"Did she?" said Alicia, a disbelieving edge to her tone.

"Oh, yes," said Katie. "Most emphatically." Alicia raised an eyebrow. Miss India Taylor, a wonderful dance teacher and a woman of very few words, was not given to effusive statements about her pupils' abilities.

"It's true, Katie, that your dancing is improving, although whether you are one of the best in the school is open to debate. In any case, it's not a matter of who is best. Pupils progress and consolidate at very different rates. But I can't deny that your audition for the Children's Royal Spectacular was very good indeed and I believe that you would be an asset to the team." She paused. "But I have to consider every aspect of your performance at the school, and your academic results do not justify your inclusion. You know the Swan policy as well as I do. Poor results in the classroom mean no public performances, professional or otherwise. So until your results show signs of improvement, reluctantly I have to say that—"

"Please, please, Miss Swan," interrupted Katie, her eyes welling with tears that glistened on her thick dark lashes. "Please don't leave me out of the team! Being part of a team would be good for me and being included would give me the incentive I need to do better in my school work. My results would improve, I promise. I'd work like a demon." She looked at Alicia from under her eyelashes. "If you would just give me one last chance, I promise I won't let you down."

Alicia looked hard at Katie. Why was it that whenever she spoke to this child, she felt as if she was watching somebody acting? It was as if Katie had lost the ability to distinguish between pretence and real life. Her instinct was to tell the girl that she had already had a chance to pull up her socks and now she must pay the price – exclusion from the Children's Royal Spectacular cast – but maybe it *was* just the spur that the child needed.

"All right," said Alicia decisively. "I'll take a chance on you, Katie. But you get one chance, and one only. The mid-term tests fall just before the final televised heat for the Spectacular. If we get that far. If you don't pass in every single subject, you're out of the team."

"Thank you, Miss Swan, I won't let you down," beamed Katie. "I'll be devoted to you forever."

"Eternal devotion isn't required, Katie, but a decent pass in algebra and comprehension is." Miss Swan looked at her watch. "Now, run along back to class. I've already kept Mrs Jones waiting, and I've got to make a quick phone call before I talk to her. On your way out, can you tell her I'm sorry for the delay and that I won't be long."

Georgia's mum was sitting in the little anteroom outside Miss Swan's office. She smiled when she saw Katie.

"How are you, Katie?" she asked.

"Very well, Mrs Jones," Katie said, smiling sweetly. "Miss Swan has just been congratulating me on my progress."

"How nice for you."

"Yes," said Katie innocently. "In fact, she said I'm so talented she wants to give me a scholarship. But I told her I didn't need one and that she should save it for someone who really does. Someone poor." She gave Mrs Jones a ravishing smile. "Someone like Georgia!" she said, as if she had just had the most delightful idea.

Georgia's mother blushed, looking disconcerted. She was surprised that Georgia had talked at school about their situation. Whenever she had tried to broach the subject of money at home and the possibility that Georgia might have to leave the Swan, her daughter had refused to discuss it.

"Oh, I do apologise, Mrs Jones!" said Katie. "That was very tactless of me. It was just that Georgia confided in me. She told me how difficult things are for you both. I didn't mean to embarrass you or myself." She looked stricken.

Mrs Jones leaned forward, thinking what a kind and delightful child Katie was and that she must do her best to encourage the friendship.

"That's all right, Katie, no offence taken. It was a lovely thought," she said, bringing the subject firmly to a close.

At that moment her mobile went off. Katie walked towards the door, and Georgia's mother gave her a little wave goodbye as she answered the phone. "Yes?" she said. She was flustered to discover it was her boss. "I booked the time off. I won't be long, I'll be back in the office before three. . . No, I'll sort it out. I've got to go." She snapped the phone shut and said angrily, "I'd tell you to stuff your stupid job if I could afford to keep Georgia at school without it!"

Georgia's mother suddenly realised that Katie hadn't left the room and immediately regretted her outburst, but Katie just said very sincerely, "I'm so sorry about your money troubles, Mrs Jones. Georgia is my absolute bestest friend. I couldn't bear it if she had to leave."

Chapter Twenty-Four

"Olivia, could you please stay behind? I want a word with you," said Sebastian Shaw.

It was the end of another class in which Olivia had sat in the corner, her face hidden by her hair, trying to pretend that she wasn't there. Sebastian waited until all the other children had gathered their belongings and headed off to the cloakrooms to change for contemporary dance or to get ready for singing. Three of the boys were going for an audition for a brand-new play at the Royal Court. It was by an exciting young female playwright who everyone said would be the next big thing.

"Olivia, Olivia, what am I going to do with you?" he asked sorrowfully. "It's clear that you are very unhappy here at the Swan but I think that you could enjoy it so much more if you would only make a little effort. You have a lovely voice, Olivia, and such expressive features. Your eyes truly are windows to your soul. If you could only overcome your shyness and use your gifts, you might become a great actress like your mother."

Olivia wanted to shout, "I don't want to be a great actress like my mother, I want to be a great tightrope-walker like my dad!" but curiosity got the better of her. Instead she asked fiercely, "You knew my mum?"

Sebastian nodded. "I taught her everything I know, and after that she started to teach *me*."

"What was she like when she was my age?" asked Olivia.

Mr Shaw smiled. "She was just like you. She was beautiful and she could be a bit frightening, and there was something a little wild about her and something a little sad, except when she laughed, and then it was as if the sun had come out. But she had one thing that I haven't yet seen in you, Olivia."

"What's that?" asked Olivia.

"She had true grit. She let nothing defeat her. Toni wasn't the most naturally gifted student we've ever had at the Swan. But she was the most determined and hard-working. She always pushed herself that little bit further than anyone else, and always picked herself up and tried again if she failed. She used to quote a famous writer called Samuel Beckett: 'Try again. Fail again. Fail better.' She took a decent talent and made it a mighty one. She was always prepared to take a risk and she never gave up."

"So you think I've given up?" asked Olivia indignantly.

"I think you gave up the day you arrived," said Sebastian Shaw gently. "You were determined not to give the Swan a chance. I also think that you're letting your unhappiness eat you up. Unhappiness is like acid. It destroys and scars." Then he smiled and added, "But maybe you will prove me wrong, Olivia. Your mother always did. I told her she didn't have what it takes to be a great classical actress, and through hard work and determination she became the greatest of her generation. Who knows, maybe if she had lived. . ."

Tears welled in Olivia's eyes. Sebastian handed her a tissue with one hand and a ticket with the other.

"What's this?" asked Olivia.

"It's a ticket for a play by Shakespeare I'm going to see tonight. *Romeo and Juliet*," said Mr Shaw. "How old are you, Olivia? Twelve?"

Olivia nodded.

"Your mother played Juliet on the West End stage when she was sixteen, only a little older than you are now. Then a few years after that she met your father. Even though she was already engaged to be married, it was love at first sight."

"She was going to marry someone else?" Olivia's eyes were wide.

Sebastian nodded. "Look, Olivia, I'd be very honoured if you would come to the theatre with me tonight to see the play. I think it might help you understand your mum and dad a little better, what their love cost, and why your father has left you and your sister here."

Olivia sniffed and Sebastian Shaw passed her another tissue. "Your father hasn't abandoned you, Olivia."

"Well, it feels like he has," she replied, and burst into such tears that Sebastian Shaw quite ran out of tissues.

Chapter Twenty-Five

There was an expectant buzz all around the theatre. Olivia leaned forwards in the box. When she had seen where they were sitting, she worried about feeling exposed and self-conscious, but the beauty of the theatre had quickly made her forget all such thoughts.

The ceiling was painted with a scene from classical Greek drama and a massive chandelier hung down from its middle, twinkling with what seemed like a thousand candles. The balconies were edged with gold gilt and cheeky little gold cherubs grinned down beatifically from above the proscenium arch over the stage. Even the battered old safety curtain was painted with garlanded shepherds and shepherdesses and darting fairies.

The gaudy gaiety reminded Olivia of the circus. She immediately felt at home.

She had only reluctantly agreed to go with Sebastian to the theatre. But the lure of hearing more about her mother, Toni, was too hard to resist. She had not been disappointed. Over a bowl of spaghetti with fresh basil in a little Italian restaurant round the corner, where the waiters had greeted Sebastian like an old friend, he had told Olivia more about her mother than Jack ever had.

"You are more like her than you could possibly imagine, Olivia. It's not just how you look and how you sound, but in other ways too," he'd said, thinking that mother and daughter were both a bit like wild ponies whose confidence you had to gain slowly and carefully.

"But she was an actor; I'm not," said Olivia, scraping her bowl of the last of her tiramisu. She found talking to Sebastian remarkably easy.

"She wasn't always. Not to start with. During her first term at the Swan, when she was seven, I could barely get her to open her mouth she was so shy in class. She'd visibly shrink if I tried to get her to stand up and say a poem. So

I simply left her alone, as I've done with you. Towards the end of the second term, we decided we were going to put on a little end-of-term show for the parents. It was a version of *Sleeping Beauty.* We had a little audition session in class, and of course all the girls wanted to play the princess. I didn't want to push Toni because I couldn't imagine she'd want to audition in front of everyone or even take part in the performance. At best, I thought she'd want to hide somewhere at the back as a courtier. But after all the other little girls had played the scene I'd chosen for them, and I said it was time to move on to the boys, Toni put up her hand.

"'What is it, Toni?' I asked.

"'I want to play the princess,' she said very firmly. Frankly, I was astonished. She had barely spoken in class for the entire year. But she stepped out to the front of the room and played the scene. It was an extraordinary performance for a seven-year-old. She had clearly studied very carefully what all the others had done, and knew where to make improvements. Of course, she got the part, and I knew then that with dedication and hard work she had the potential to be a great actor. Eventually she was."

Then Sebastian had looked at his watch and nodded to a waiter for the bill. "We must hurry or we'll be late for the theatre."

They had taken their seats, and as the house lights started to dim Olivia felt the same excitement that she felt at the start of a circus performance. The royal-blue curtains across the stage swung open. Suddenly Olivia was transported back to Italy on a hot summer's day. She leaned further forwards. She could almost smell the bright colours. At first she found the language difficult to understand, but gradually her ear adjusted and it grew easier. She watched the preparations for the Capulets' party and enjoyed the banter between Romeo and his friend, Mercutio. They reminded her of Tom and William.

When Juliet made her first entrance, Olivia was surprised how young and fragile she was. She wondered what it must have been like to live in those times when you had to obey your parents and a girl just a few years older than she was now would be married off to someone they'd chosen for her.

Then the party began and Romeo and Juliet glimpsed each other across the room crowded with dancers. Romeo breathed the words, *"O! She doth teach the torches to burn bright."* Olivia felt her heart flutter inside her chest as if it was a bird trying to get out.

Romeo approached Juliet for the first time:

"If I profane with my unworthiest hand
This holy shrine, the gentle sin is this;
My lips, two blushing pilgrims, ready stand
To smooth that rough touch with a tender kiss."

For a moment, Olivia suddenly thought about her parents' first meeting, and then she was completely swept away by the story again. Romeo and Juliet were secretly married without their parents' knowledge, Romeo was banished after killing Juliet's cousin, Tybalt, and Juliet was forced by her parents to prepare to marry the man they had chosen for her, Paris. It was as if Olivia was experiencing the play with every sense, and she completely forgot that she was sitting in a theatre in the heart of London and felt instead as if she were Juliet in Verona hundreds of years ago.

During the interval she spoke very little, eager for the play to resume. When, after the final tragedy of the young lovers' deaths, the play finished, Olivia sat in dazed silence, tears pouring down her cheeks. For a long time she couldn't speak. Sebastian waited patiently and just handed her tissues.

Finally she sniffed, turned to Sebastian and said, "It was wonderful. Thank you. I loved every minute. I had no idea that the theatre could be so amazing."

Sebastian smiled. "As good as the circus?"

"Totally, but in a different way," said Olivia, surprising herself.

"They both have their strengths," said Sebastian.

Olivia nodded, and as she did so an idea popped into her head.

Chapter Twenty-Six

When they arrived back at the Swan after the theatre, Sebastian pressed a copy of *Romeo and Juliet* into Olivia's hand, telling her it was a present, before he made his goodbyes and left to walk around the corner to his flat.

Olivia stood alone in the large foyer of the Swan. She liked the school best at night when it was empty, so different from the hustle and bustle of the day. Then it was full of people and energy, and a different noise – from choral speaking to tap-dancing – drifted from behind every door. It felt so peaceful at night.

She headed up the wide sweeping staircase towards the upper floor where Alicia had her flat. But when she reached the first floor, she stopped and turned back and, leaning over the balcony, she opened the play. She started to speak:

> *"O Romeo, Romeo! Wherefore art thou,
> Romeo?
> Deny thy father, and refuse thy name;
> Or, if thou wilt not, be but sworn by love,
> And I'll no longer be a Capulet."*

If her grandmother or Sebastian Shaw had been watching, they would have sworn they were seeing a ghost.

The next day Tom and Olivia were practising in the room at the top of the school.

"That's epic, you're coming on brilliantly," said Olivia, watching Tom walk the wire to the point where it touched the ledge of the open window in the upper rehearsal room. He leapt gracefully to the ground and wiped the perspiration from his forehead.

Olivia suddenly spun round quickly to face the little observation window, but there was nobody there.

"What's up?" asked Tom.

"I sometimes get the feeling we're being spied on by somebody," said Olivia. "We should be more careful about pulling the blind right down."

"Are Katie and her coven still bothering you?" asked Tom.

Olivia ignored the question and quickly changed the subject. "You're getting so good, I was wondering whether we might work up a little double act. Nothing too complicated."

"Whoa, Olivia Marvell. I'm just a beginner. I'm nowhere near your league."

"You're improving every day. My dad would say you're a complete natural. You really are making amazing progress," said Olivia.

"That's because I've got a brilliant teacher, who also happens to be a slave driver," grinned Tom.

Olivia blushed with pleasure. Since she had been at the Swan, she had forgotten what it was like to be praised. Then she said casually, "Have you read *Romeo and Juliet*?"

"Bits. We don't do it in acting class until we're in Year Eleven. But I've seen the movie. It's fantastic, and I saw the Royal Shakespeare Company do it on stage and that was wonderful too." He looked at Olivia's expectant face. "Why do you want to know?"

Olivia suddenly felt impossibly shy. Her words came out in a rush.

"It's just I went to the theatre last night to see it with Mr Shaw, and when I came home I read some of the speeches; acting it out made me feel just like I feel inside when I'm on the tightrope and doing something really difficult really well. It's as if nothing else in the world matters except the moment that you're caught up in and I just wondered . . . I just wondered—" Olivia broke off, embarrassed. "No, it's a silly idea. . ."

"You can't stop now," said Tom, "but if it really sucks, I'll tell you."

"Well," said Olivia nervously, "when I was thinking about the play, I thought that the feelings Romeo and Juliet have, and the feeling of being on a tightrope, are rather similar. It's all risky and dangerous, scary and off-kilter, as if you're wobbling about and yet perfectly balanced at the same time, and I just thought. . ." Olivia faltered again.

"Spit it out, Liv!" said Tom impatiently.

"I just wondered what it would be like to act out the moment when they first meet at the masked ball, or the balcony scene, or something, on the tightrope."

Olivia looked up at Tom from under her hair, wondering nervously what he was going to think, but Tom looked interested. "With the words or without?"

"Whichever way works best. Maybe some words, but not all of them. It'd have to be a perfect mix of words and movement. I don't know, we'd have to try it and see."

"But that means we'd both have to tightrope-walk, speak and act all at the same time," said Tom slowly.

"Yes," said Olivia. "We would." Then she added enthusiastically, "I don't think it's ever been done before. At least, not in the circus."

"I can see why not," said Tom. "Doing one of those things well is hard enough; trying to do all three is insane."

Olivia's face fell.

Tom spoke gently. "Look, Liv, I can probably do the Shakespeare bit OK. Just about. Speaking Shakespeare's really hard. But I can still barely tightrope-walk. And although you can do the tightrope-walking and acrobatics brilliantly, I've yet to hear you open your mouth in acting class, though I've always thought it requires an immense talent to make yourself appear as invisible as you manage every lesson. And aren't you the girl who not so long ago told us all that acting was silly?"

Olivia glared at him, and said, "Well, it can be. When it's done badly. But Mr Shaw's got a point. Circus and acting have got a lot in common. Actually, I've decided I quite like acting." She paused, and then added, "I just don't like doing it in front of other people." Tom started to laugh, but he stopped when he saw Olivia's serious face. "Trying to act in front of other people makes me feel as if there's nowhere to hide, that the people watching can see right inside me."

"Yes," said Tom, "that's exactly what it's like. Acting's scary, but after a while you just forget that people are watching you and it's like shedding one layer of skin after another until you're completely naked."

"Like a snake," said Olivia.

"Yes," said Tom, "although not the poisonous kind, unless you're Katie Wilkes-Cox." He grinned. "Come on, dark horse, let's give it a whirl. Maybe we'll be better together than we are alone."

"That's what a double act is. By trusting each other completely and doing what you do best, but also by being generous, you make the other person look even better. In a true double act, one and one doesn't make two, it makes three."

"I believe you," said Tom, "but I'm very gullible." He grinned. "All right, then, let's give it a go."

Olivia beamed at him. Then, from somewhere at the bottom of the school, came the distant sound of excited screams and shouts of congratulation.

"The results for the Children's Royal Spectacular auditions must be up on the notice board," said Tom. "Come on, let's go have a look."

Olivia shook her head. "I didn't audition for the silly show, remember. I'm not interested."

Tom caught her hand. "But I did, and now we're a double act, you've got to support me in everything I do."

Chapter Twenty-Seven

There was quite a crowd around the notice board, peering at the list of names. Eel was dancing a little jig, and when she saw Olivia, she rushed to hug her sister.

"I'm going to dance on TV and in front of the Queen!" she said excitedly.

"So am I!" said Tom, with a whoop. "Well, the TV bit's certain; we've just got to be so royally good that the public votes for us as the act the Queen most wants to see."

"Congrats, I'm really pleased for both of you," said Olivia, and she was, but she couldn't help feeling a bit lonely, an outsider at these celebrations.

"We must tell Dad; he won't want to miss seeing me dance," cried Eel.

"No, he won't," agreed Olivia, and she hugged Eel again. "Dad will be very proud of you, Eel, and. . ." she paused, ". . .and if Mum was still alive she would be too."

They rushed upstairs to Alicia's flat and dialled the mobile number that Jack had left them. But instead of hearing his cheery, "Hello, girls," all they heard was an impersonal voice telling them: "The number you have dialled has not been recognised. Please check and try again."

Eel burst into tears. "His phone's been cut off because he can't pay the bill."

"I'm sure it's just a mistake and we'll hear from him soon," said Olivia soothingly. But the knot of anxiety in her stomach tightened. She remembered listening to Jack talk to some of the other circus performers around the fire late one evening. He had been describing his preparations for his dangerous stunts, and how in the few weeks before a stunt you had to close down the rest of your life and concentrate on nothing but the stunt ahead of you. She recalled his face, contorted with fear, the last time he tried to walk the high-wire, and she shivered.

"Are you OK, Livy?" asked Eel anxiously.

"Yep," said Olivia. "Let's go find Tom."

Alicia walked into the room at that moment. "What are you up to with Tom?" she asked with interest, pleased to think that Olivia might at last be settling down.

"Nothing. We're not doing anything," said Olivia, turning pink and glaring at her grandmother stonily in the hope of preventing further questioning. If her gran found out about the high-wire walking, Olivia felt certain she would ban it.

Alicia took a deep breath and counted to five. "Olivia, my dear, I wasn't trying to pry. I'm just glad that you've made a friend."

"Oh," said Olivia, embarrassed at her overreaction. "I'm sorry, Gran, but I've got to go."

"Why don't you just tell her about the tightrope-walking?" asked Eel as they headed down the stairs.

"Because she'd never understand in a million years," replied Olivia.

Georgia stood all alone by the notice board, biting her lip. Everyone else had drifted away to celebrate or to commiserate. She peered again at the list pinned to the wall. There was her name in black letters. It wasn't a mistake.

Miss Swan had taken her to one of the rehearsal rooms alone and coaxed a performance out of her. Georgia didn't think she'd been very good but clearly Miss Swan had taken a chance on her again. This time she vowed she would make her proud.

But she didn't feel as thrilled as she would have done just a few weeks ago. Then she would have been delighted that all her hard work, and her mum's, was starting to pay off. She would have loved to see her mum's tired face light up with pride. But instead she just felt completely numb, because there at the bottom of the list was another name: Katie Wilkes-Cox.

When she had run towards the notice board, she had silently been begging: "Please, please, let my name be there and please, please, let Katie's not." But she wasn't surprised at what she found; for the last few hours, Katie had been wandering around with her cat's-got-the-cream smile, making Georgia suspect that somehow Katie already knew she had a place in the cast. Katie hadn't even bothered to come and look at the list.

Georgia rested her hot forehead against the notice board. She realised that Katie made her feel like a helpless little mouse caught between a cat's paws and she was beginning to hate her for it. She couldn't think why she had ever wanted to be her friend. She supposed that she must have been seduced by Katie's pretty face, long golden hair and air of easy entitlement. How she had longed to be the chosen one, how she had savoured every smile tossed in her direction and every conspiratorial giggle. Georgia had never felt like the sort of person who belonged anywhere, so being part of Katie's gang had made her feel special.

But Georgia increasingly felt that being Katie's friend was like being under a curse. And it was all her own fault. If she had never bragged and made up that silly, thoughtless lie about New York, a lie that had somehow led to another lie and then another, she wouldn't have Katie on her back now, constantly testing her and nagging her to bring in the topaz ring to prove how rich she was. The only good thing, thought Georgia, was that although Katie obviously had her suspicions that Georgia had been lying about being rich, she clearly wasn't entirely certain of the truth and Georgia was doing her best to keep her guessing – only yesterday she had raided her piggy bank for the last few pounds that she had been saving to buy a Christmas present for her mum and used it to get everyone ice creams in the park after school. Ones with chocolate flakes too, as if money was no object!

She heard a noise behind her and spun round. Katie was standing there, a smile playing at the corners of her mouth.

"Hello, little Miss Georgia Jones," she said, in a voice that dripped with menace.

Georgia stared at her feet.

"It's very rude not to answer when someone says hello to you, Georgia – even when you're a multi-billionaire. Anyone would think you didn't like me. But I *luurve* you, Georgia Jones, and your mummy seems to like me very much."

"What are you talking about, Katie?" asked Georgia hotly.

"We were having a lovely cosy chat this morning, just outside Miss Swan's office."

Georgia's heart sank right down into her toes. So her mum must have come to give notice. She would have to leave the Swan! Her throat felt as if something hard was lodged there. "What did my mum say?" she whispered.

"Oh, nothing much," said Katie, airily. "Just that she was so poor you were going to have to leave unless old Swan gave you a scholarship, and we all know that she's never going to do that. Not in a million years." Katie looked at her watch. "Oh, look! I'm going to be late to meet the others. I'm really looking forward to telling everyone your mum's sob story about being so poor. It'll rock."

"You don't have to tell them," said Georgia. "Please don't be nasty, Katie."

"What will you do for me, if I don't?" asked the other girl.

"Whatever you want," whispered Georgia, refusing to meet Katie's eye.

"All right," said Katie with a smile. "I won't tell everyone that little Miss Georgia Jones is a compulsive fibber and really, *really* poor. But you'll have to do some things for me, and you can start with my maths homework."

When Georgia got home that evening her mum was waiting for her, clearly bursting with excitement. She had cooked Georgia's favourite food: shepherd's pie with green peas, and toffee cheesecake for pudding.

"Guess what?" said Mrs Jones. Georgia said nothing; she wasn't in the mood for playing games.

"Are you tired, darling?" asked her mum. "Sometimes I think the Swan school day is far too long. But I've got news, great news, that will perk you up!"

Georgia still said nothing, but her mother didn't notice. She rushed on. "I went to see Miss Swan today and she's very kindly awarded you a full scholarship. Isn't it wonderful! You can stay on at the Swan with all your friends and carry on your training. I thought maybe you'd like to invite a friend over for a sleepover at the weekend to celebrate. Maybe Katie? She's so lovely. She told me you confided in her. She sounds like a real friend."

To her puzzlement, Georgia burst into tears and rushed upstairs, refusing to come down to eat her supper. Later Mrs Jones went upstairs and sat on the edge of Georgia's bed, stroking her hair gently.

"Georgia, is everything all right at school? You would tell me, darling, if you were unhappy at the Swan or being bullied, wouldn't you? We could sort it out, whatever it is that's going on."

For a moment, Georgia wanted to sit up and fling her arms around her mum and tell her everything that was happening and how unhappy Katie was making her. But she knew her mother had enough on her plate with her job and her money worries. Besides, it would also mean telling her mum about how she had lied about them going to New York and being rich, and she couldn't bear the thought of her mum being disappointed in her. So she said nothing and just curled up into a miserable little ball instead.

Chapter Twenty-Eight

Miss Swan stood in front of the assembled school, which was gathered once again in the theatre. As always, she looked around the room before speaking.

She was pleased to see that Olivia was looking a little more cheerful and quite clearly had struck up a real friendship with Tom McCavity. She wondered what on earth the two of them talked about together, but she was delighted to see the bloom in her granddaughter's cheeks.

Georgia looked more pale and wan than ever. Her marks in her schoolwork seemed to be suffering, too. Alicia was surprised. She had thought that getting a scholarship would have given Georgia confidence but it seemed to have had the opposite effect. She wondered if the child was ill.

Katie, on the other hand, was blooming. She looked glossier than ever and she had been as good as her word when it came to pulling her socks up academically. Her homework had been coming in on time and some of it had been very good indeed. Sometimes, thought Alicia, it was right to go against your instincts.

She cleared her throat.

"Good morning. And it *is* a good morning. As I'm sure you all know by now, the Swan is through to the final stages of the competition for a place in the Children's Royal Spectacular. Our performance was the hit of last week's televised show! Congratulations to everyone involved. We're all very proud of you and we're confident that we can make it to the show in front of the Queen, provided everyone keeps working hard over the next two weeks. There will be no let-up in rehearsals and, as I'm sure you have all remembered, mid-term tests start tomorrow. I know you will all do your best.

"Now to other news: I'm delighted to announce that one of our most talented and hard-working students, our very popular head girl, Abbie Cardew, has been cast as Liesl in

The Sound of Music! I know that you will all join with me in congratulating her."

The entire theatre broke into cheers. Abbie blushed, looking pleased.

"Right, everyone," continued the headmistress. "There's lots to be done, so back to work!"

Olivia was alone in her form room, using the computer. She shouldn't have been there as it was out of bounds at lunchtime while the mid-term tests were on, but she was desperate to try and find out some news of Jack. His silence was becoming increasingly ominous. He had sent them a postcard saying that he would be away for a little while, but three weeks had gone by since then, and she could see that even Alicia was worried by his lack of contact.

But Olivia had even more reason for anxiety; she was certain that Jack was about to undertake a major stunt, something so amazing, so dangerous, that it would grab the attention of the world's media.

She had been putting "Jack Marvell" and "Great Marvello" into search engines for twenty minutes and, although they had thrown up thousands of results about past feats, there was no whisper about an up-coming stunt. It was something of a relief. She shut down the computer and was just about to leave when she heard a noise outside the door and the unmistakable sound of Katie Wilkes-Cox's voice. Katie was the last person Olivia wanted to catch her in the room. She squeezed herself in the small space between the desk and the radiator just as the door opened.

"Katie, please don't do this," whispered Georgia urgently as they entered the room.

"Don't be dumb, Georgia. I can't risk failing the maths exam. I'll get kicked off the Children's Spectacular team. Old Swan made that quite clear. Which sucks, by the way. I'm clearly one of the stars, so what does it matter that I can't do algebra?"

"You could do it if you only tried. You're not stupid," said Georgia seriously.

Katie spun round furiously. "No, Georgia Jones, I'm not stupid. In fact, I'm rather smart. Which is why I'm going to sneak a look at the questions and you're going to tell me the answers."

"But you won't be able to show your

workings out," said Georgia.

"It doesn't matter. Just as long as I pass," said Katie impatiently. "Look, are you going to help me find the test or do I have to reveal your nasty little secret to the whole school?"

"Cheating is wrong," said Georgia, sounding near to tears.

"Oh, and lying isn't?" said Katie. She opened the cupboard. "Look, here are the test papers. We'll take one. Nobody will notice it's missing. They always have more copies than they need. And then you can work out the answers for me tonight, come in early, and I'll learn them in time for the test after break. And make sure that when you do the test yourself you put in some stupid mistakes like you do on the homework so the answers aren't the same."

"I can't do this, Katie, I *won't* do it. . ." whimpered Georgia.

"Oh, but you will, little Miss Georgia Jones, you will. And by the way, you'd better bring in your mum's famous ring. Next Wednesday, I think, the day we get the test results. I can't imagine why, but it appears that some of the others are having serious doubts about whether it really exists."

They left the room. Olivia waited for a moment, shocked by what she'd heard, and deep in thought. She didn't know what to do. If she did nothing, Katie might get away with cheating and would also continue to bully poor Georgia. But if she went and told Miss Swan what she'd heard, she would be guilty of snitching and she wouldn't just get Katie into deep trouble, but Georgia too.

She'd also have to explain what she'd been doing in the room in the first place and things wouldn't look good for her. She wouldn't put it past Katie to twist the truth and say that she and Georgia had discovered *Olivia* in the act of cheating. Olivia felt really anxious and she was more worried still when she tried to creep out of the room unseen only to find Katie lolling against the wall opposite, smiling.

"Well, well, well. I had a feeling there was someone else in the room so I thought I'd just hang around. Lucky I did." She leaned forward and hissed, "You dare mention a word about this, Liver Marvell, and I'll clip your wings forever." Then with a toss of her hair she was gone.

Olivia stared after her. She had thought

Georgia was weak for allowing herself to be manipulated by Katie, but she wondered if she was really any better. She felt a real wave of sympathy for Georgia.

Chapter Twenty-Nine

The music came to an end, and the children took their bow. Alicia Swan stood up.

"Thank you very much everyone. That was excellent. Rehearsal dismissed. Please go back and join your Wednesday afternoon classes, they'll be starting in five minutes."

The children filed away. When the last child had gone, Alicia turned to the little group sitting in the stalls. It was made up of several members of staff, including Mr Shaw and Stella Hanbury, as well as the head girl, Abbie, who had also been invited to the rehearsal. There was a tiny silence and then Alicia said crisply, "So, do you see what I mean?"

"It's good, very good," ventured Sebastian Shaw.

"Oh, yes, it's good. Excellent even, but it's not *excellent enough.* At least, not to get us through to the finals. It doesn't have that indefinable spark. It lacks something, but I don't know what it is," said Alicia.

She turned to Abbie. "I invited you, my dear, because I know that you have a good eye, and you are young and so have a different perspective. Do you know what it is that is missing?"

Abbie blushed. It was thrilling that Miss Swan thought that her opinion mattered, but a bit daunting too. She was worried that she might seem rude if she told the truth. She looked into Miss Swan's expectant face and summoned all her courage.

"Originality," she said, stuttering over the word. "What it lacks is originality." Then she added quickly, "Of course, it's very good, just as you'd expect from the Swan, but that's part of the problem, it is exactly what people have come to expect from us. It's not the least bit surprising. . ." Her voice trailed off and she felt embarrassed for speaking so plainly in front of her teachers, but she saw them nodding and Alicia Swan's face had cracked into a wide smile.

"You're quite right, Abbie. I'm so pleased I asked you to join us. You've cleverly put your finger on the problem. What we've produced is of the highest quality, but it's way too predictable. If the Swan is going to win a top-three place in the final, then we are going to have to come up with something that will surprise everyone. Something that nobody would expect from us."

"But there are only two days to go!" said Stella Hanbury anxiously. "Surely it's too late to change things now?"

"It's never too late," said Alicia. "I only wish I knew what to change it *to*. All ideas will be gratefully received." She looked at her watch. "Classes are about to start; we must all go. But now we've identified the problem we need to come up with some solutions without delay."

Chapter Thirty

As soon as the rehearsal ended, Katie detached herself from the others and ran quickly to the stairs that led to the upper rehearsal room. She peered furtively through the observation window. Just as she had expected, it was empty. Katie smiled to herself. All her weeks of spying on Olivia and Tom were proving useful. She was glad that she had kept their secret to herself.

It was payback time for Miss Olivia Marvell. She didn't trust her. She had seen Olivia's face when the maths test results had been announced and Katie had come top of the class. "A quite remarkable performance," said Mr Baldwin, the maths teacher, with a slightly puzzled air. For a moment Katie had thought that Olivia was going to say something there and then. She couldn't live with the risk. Olivia wasn't popular, but she wasn't disliked the way she had been at the start of term, particularly now that she was friends with Tom McCavity, whom everyone liked. But there was also something about her quiet, serious manner that carried authority. Something had to be done about her, something that would totally destroy her credibility in case she had any ideas about snitching on Katie. Katie smiled. She had thought of just the thing.

Katie walked over to the cupboard where Olivia hid the suitcase with her high-wire. She put her hand in her pocket, pulled out a pair of diamond and pearl earrings and then slipped them into the bottom of Olivia's case. Katie left the room quickly and ran lightly down the stairs, mingling with the throng that was beginning to gather on the landing below. Nobody saw her come down the stairs and rejoin the group of shrieking children, nobody except Georgia, who noticed Katie's strange cat-like smile.

Katie saw her looking. "Say anything, and you're pet food," she said in a threatening whisper.

Georgia was puzzled. What could

Katie have been doing up there that was so mysterious?

At that moment Miss Hanbury arrived with Abbie, who liked to observe and help out in classes whenever she had a free period. Miss Hanbury shooed them all up the stairs towards the upper rehearsal room for voice class. As she entered the room, she sniffed and announced, "Yuk! Sweaty bodies," before striding over to the windows and flinging them wide open. "That's better."

She turned to the class. "Please put any valuables on the window sill. We don't want any jewellery getting in the way or change jingling in pockets. All on the window sill, please."

Georgia felt in her pocket for her mum's garnet and topaz ring, and ran over and placed it carefully in the corner of the window sill. She had borrowed it from her mum's dressing table without asking, and now she fervently wished that she hadn't. Nobody, least of all Katie, had seemed particularly interested when she'd shown it to everyone during first break. They had all been much more interested in Katie's mum's diamond and pearl earrings, which had made the little ring look a bit pathetic.

Georgia knew that Katie had brought the earrings in deliberately to make the ring look insignificant, but she was just pleased that for once Katie didn't needle her about it. It was as if Katie was distracted by something more important. Whatever it was, Georgia was grateful; she was desperate for the day to end so she could get the ring safely back on her mum's dressing table before she noticed it had gone.

"Your mum's ring really is pretty," said Aeysha, placing a little pearl necklace she usually wore around her neck next to it. Several other children put small piles of change on the window sill.

As soon as everybody was back in their places, Miss Hanbury said, "Right everybody, let's begin. Breathe in. . ."

Chapter Thirty-One

They had just finished the first exercise when Katie raised her hand. "Sorry, Miss Hanbury," she said sweetly, holding up her hand as if she was clutching something in it. "I've just remembered I had my mum's diamond and pearl earrings in my pocket. They're very expensive, I mustn't lose them. My mum would kill me."

"Well, hurry up and put them on the window sill with everybody else's valuables, Katie," said Miss Hanbury impatiently. "You really shouldn't bring such precious things to school."

Katie ran to the window and appeared to place something on the sill, but nobody took much notice of her because Miss Hanbury was already in full flow, explaining the next breathing exercise. Katie returned meekly to her place and lay down, feeling smug. Everything was going to plan.

The class continued for thirty minutes, during which everybody worked hard. "Right," said Miss Hanbury. "We'll take our normal five-minute break and then we'll start again." She swept out of the room, which emptied after her as the pupils went to get a drink or use the lavatory. Only Olivia, Georgia and Katie were left.

"Come along, little Miss Jones," said Katie.

Georgia slid down the wall and shook her head, not looking at Katie.

Katie loomed over her. "Georgia, move it. I told you to come with me." Georgia stood up reluctantly, still avoiding Katie's gaze.

"Georgia, you don't have to do everything Katie tells you to," said Olivia quietly. Georgia flung her a grateful smile.

"But she likes to do what I say because she knows what's good for her," said Katie. Georgia turned pink and followed her meekly. At the door, Katie turned back and looked at Olivia. She smiled nastily and spat out, "Loser. That's what you are, Liver Marvell. A loser."

Georgia followed Katie numbly. She thought back over the term. It had begun with such promise; how had everything gone so wrong? She knew that she had acted like a complete coward and she felt tired, and empty, and close to tears. She was overcome by a sudden rush of guilt at how much pain they had all inflicted on Olivia, and she thought that if she was having a miserable time, how much worse must Olivia feel. She went to turn back, but Katie clutched her firmly by the hand and pulled her down the stairs as if she were a rag doll.

Chapter Thirty-Two

Everyone returned to the room after the break, chattering and laughing. "Right," said Miss Hanbury, clapping her hands, "let's recommence. Back in the same places, please."

"Miss Hanbury!" Katie's hand was in the air. "Miss Hanbury!"

"What is it now, Katie?" asked Miss Hanbury, her voice tinged with impatience.

"It's my earrings, Miss."

"What about them?" snapped Miss Hanbury.

"They're gone!"

"What do you mean, *gone*?"

"They're not here, Miss. I put them on the window sill." Katie looked around at the class, her blue eyes wide. "You saw me, didn't you?"

she pleaded and several people nodded, even Miss Hanbury. "But they're not here now."

"They must be," said Miss Hanbury, striding over to the window sill. But although Aeysha's chain, Georgia's ring and the little piles of money were still there, the earrings had gone.

"Somebody has taken them," said Katie, and her eyes filled with tears. She gave a little gasp. "Miss Hanbury, it must be the same person who took all those other things, including the gold chain your fiancé gave you." She paused dramatically before adding, "That means the thief must be in this room. She must be one of us." Everyone including Miss Hanbury stared at her, shocked.

"Or he," said Tom. "The thief could just as easily be a boy."

"Oh, I'd never wear diamond earrings. They don't suit me," said William Todd. There was a ripple of laughter.

Miss Hanbury glared round the room. "Has anybody seen Katie's earrings?"

Everyone shook their heads and muttered, "No."

"You do realise how serious this is, don't

you?" said Miss Hanbury, her face grim.

"Please, Miss Hanbury," said Katie. "I know they were there on the window sill before break because I almost put them in my pocket when I went downstairs. If only I had taken them with me!"

"Well, we must search for them," said Miss Hanbury. "Can everybody please look around carefully in case they've fallen on the floor." Everyone started looking but without much hope of finding the earrings. Katie and Aeysha were by the cupboard.

"Look in there, Aeysha," said Katie nonchalantly. Aeysha opened the door.

"There's only an old suitcase that someone's left," said Aeysha. She went to close the door.

"Might be worth looking inside," whispered Katie firmly.

Aeysha shrugged and pulled the case out of the cupboard. As she did so, Katie moved towards the other side of the room. Olivia suddenly realised what was happening and that her tightrope wire was about to be discovered.

"Hey, that's mine, leave it alone!" she shouted. But it was too late. Aeysha already had the suitcase open and had tipped it upside down.

Out fell the wire in a heap on the floor, swiftly followed by the earrings. For a second, everyone stared at the earrings and then everyone looked at Olivia.

Olivia put her hands to her face and took a step backwards.

Chapter Thirty-Three

"I didn't . . . I wouldn't. . ." Olivia's voice faltered. The sea of faces all around her were either hostile or, in the case of Tom and Georgia, puzzled.

"Is this your suitcase?" asked Miss Hanbury.

Olivia nodded mutely.

"Can you explain how Katie's earrings came to be inside it?"

Olivia shook her head miserably.

"Katie, let me get this clear because it's important," said Miss Hanbury. "You are quite certain that the earrings were on the sill before break but they weren't there afterwards?"

"Yes, Miss Hanbury."

"So they must have gone missing during

break." Several people murmured their agreement.

"Did everybody leave during break?" People started to say, "Yes," before Miss Hanbury interrupted. "Perhaps it would be easier to ask if anybody stayed here during the break?"

There was a tense silence and then Olivia said in a very small voice, "Yes, I did. I was here."

There was a buzz of excitement in the room.

"She's the thief, Miss Hanbury. She took my earrings and all those other things that have gone missing too," said Katie.

Several others shook their heads in disbelief. Miss Hanbury looked worried.

"Olivia, I hope for your sake there has been a dreadful mistake of some kind. Sit down, everybody, and don't move. Abbie, you wait here with the children and don't let anyone leave. I'm going to get Miss Swan."

Everyone shuffled around the suitcase and its spilled contents as if trying not to examine the evidence too closely, and found themselves a space to sit down. Olivia moved towards the window and sat there all alone. Everyone else was at the other end of the room. It was as if she had some terribly contagious disease. Nobody would look her in the eye, except Tom, who suddenly stood up, detached himself from the rest of the group and walked over to Olivia. He sat down next to her and squeezed her hand.

"I don't believe you're a thief, Liv," he said loudly.

Olivia gave him a wan little smile, then she closed her eyes and leaned back against the wall.

Chapter Thirty-Four

All was silence in the room, but it wasn't a comfortable silence; it was like the quiet before the first thunderclap of a terrific storm. Suddenly the silence was shattered. There was a flap of wings, a sudden "Caw" and then a flash of black and white feathers in the window. A bird swooped down on to the sill and grabbed something in its beak. There was a glint of topaz and garnet as it flew off.

There was a shocked silence. Nobody could quite believe what they had just witnessed. Then Georgia stood up and ran to the window. "My ring. That bird has stolen my mother's ring!" she cried. She burst into tears.

Everyone stood up and crowded around the window, making Olivia and Tom shuffle aside. The bird did a circuit in the sky and then it swooped down and sat on the edge of the building, the ring still quite clearly visible in its beak. It eyed the children cheekily as if it was taunting them by being so close and yet so far. Then it hopped down into its nest, deposited the ring, and flew off again.

"It's put the ring in its nest!" shouted William. "We'll have to go next door and get on to the roof."

"We can't," said Aeysha. "The building is derelict and it's all boarded up. There's no way in."

Georgia was still sobbing quietly. "I'll have to tell my mum I've lost her ring and she'll be so disappointed in me. I've let her down." Aeysha put an arm around her comfortingly.

The group was suddenly alerted by a noise behind them. They turned round. Olivia walked towards them, her dark eyes burning in her white face, tugging one end of the wire. The other she had already attached to the hook by the door. There was something about her face that made the crowd of children part immediately to let her pass. She strode to the window sill, leaned out and expertly threw the wire so that the hook at the end slid over the spike on the roof of the building next door. Then she tugged at the rope to make sure there was no slack, and jumped on to the window sill. Tom moved swiftly close beside her.

"No, Liv," he said fiercely. "You can't do it, it's too dangerous."

"No, Olivia, no," cried Abbie, suddenly realising what was about to happen. But it was too late. Before anyone could stop her, Olivia had stepped nimbly over the edge of the sill and was perched on the wire above thirty metres of thin air. Aeysha screamed, and several others gasped or cried out.

"Quiet," said Tom. "She needs absolute quiet." The ensuing silence was so intense it was as if everyone in the room were holding their breath. Even Katie looked scared.

But Olivia moved lithely across the narrow gap between the two buildings as if she was taking a stroll in the park, seemingly oblivious to the dizzyingly drop beneath her. She reached the edge of the derelict building and stepped without difficulty over the ledge and on to the roof. Everybody in the room clapped and whooped admiringly.

Olivia tried to block out the noise. She had to keep concentrating. She looked around to check that the bird was nowhere near, then she leaned over the parapet and reached down into the nest. She felt around with her fingers and touched something. It wasn't a ring, it was a bracelet. She held it up.

"It's Aeysha's bracelet, I recognise it," shouted William. Olivia found something else. It was a thin gold chain.

"I'm sure that's Miss Hanbury's chain," cried Aeysha. Katie was beginning to look uncomfortable. Georgia bit her lip. Olivia was feeling around in the nest. She pulled up her hand and called out, "I've got your ring, Georgia."

Georgia cried out in relief. "Oh, thank you, Olivia! Thank you so much," she said.

Olivia continued to feel around in the nest and soon she had filled her pockets with assorted coins and bits of jewellery. A plop of water landed on her head. She looked up. It was starting to rain. Great big spots. The wire would become slippery very quickly. She climbed back over the parapet and on to the ledge. She took a deep breath and once more stepped into thin air.

Twenty-five pairs of eyes watched her intently. She edged her way back towards them, trying to ignore their tense, expectant faces and the terrible drop below her. She thought of nothing except taking one step after another. She could hear her own heart thumping. She was just centimetres away from the sill when the door of the rehearsal room flew open abruptly and in strode Miss Swan, followed by Miss Hanbury and Eel.

Olivia stood still as a statue. For a second, grandmother and granddaughter stared at each other, wide-eyed and white-faced. Then the bird, angry at having its space invaded and nest ransacked, swooped down from the sky and dived straight at Olivia.

"No!" shouted Alicia desperately. Eel screamed and everybody else cried out. Olivia tried to block out the noise but her concentration was broken, and the wire was wet and treacherously slippery. She took one final step towards safety, and as she did so she stumbled and began to fall. . .

Chapter Thirty-Five

There was a terrible silence in the rehearsal room. Everyone's faces were grave. Several people were crying with shock. Alicia had turned the colour of chalk, Miss Hanbury was shaking and Eel's face was wet with tears. She was sobbing uncontrollably and being comforted by Aeysha and William. Katie looked seriously scared.

"You could have died, Olivia," whispered Alicia, and she shivered as if she was watching Olivia's body tumble off the wire and plummet to the ground like a stone.

"Yes, I could have done, but I didn't. It was just lucky that Tom pulled me over the window ledge." She grinned at him. "Thanks, partner."

"You fell over it all by yourself, more like," said Tom, rubbing his bruised head ruefully.

"I just broke your fall."

"Olivia," said Alicia, "you must promise me that you'll never do anything so dangerous again."

"I promise, Gran, I'll never do anything so dangerous again . . . unless I feel that I have to," said Olivia firmly.

Alicia said nothing, she just looked at her granddaughter with a wry smile on her face. She knew she had met her match. She also knew now where Olivia had been during her long absences. She felt guilty that the child had thought she'd needed to keep such a secret from her.

"Miss Swan," said Miss Hanbury apologetically. "We must clear up the matter of the earrings."

"Ah, yes, the earrings," said Alicia, her eyes flicking around the room and coming to rest on Katie. The girl tried to hold her gaze but couldn't. She flinched; Miss Swan's gaze was as penetrating as a searchlight. Alicia walked over to the table where the pearl and diamond earrings rested alongside all the money and jewellery that Olivia had rescued from the nest.

"If I'm not mistaken," said Alicia, "all

the items reported missing are on the table. So that means the thief we thought was operating in the school was in fact our feathered friend here. Some birds are well known for their love of shiny things and this one has proved itself a most skilful thief." Everyone nodded.

"But," continued Alicia smoothly, "that still doesn't account for the missing earrings, does it?" Everyone looked puzzled. "It seems to me that there are only two explanations. One is that we have two thieves: the bird, who we know took all the other things, and Olivia, who has been accused of taking Katie's earrings. It does seem rather mysterious that she took the earrings, and only the earrings, and left behind all the other valuables that were there for the taking on the sill."

Alicia let what she had said sink in, and then she continued: "The other explanation is that we have only one thief: the bird, who is quite clearly guilty, and something else entirely is going on with the earrings." She paused, and then she said pointedly, "Perhaps they were never missing at all."

A little gasp escaped from Katie's lips, a sort of half-cry and half-whimper.

"Whatever the truth, I intend to get to the bottom of it," continued the headmistress.

Miss Swan looked at Olivia and Katie. "You two are to come with me to my office. If anyone has any further information that they would like to offer, perhaps they would speak now."

Chapter Thirty-Six

The silence seemed to go on for eternity. Alicia looked around the room. "Anyone?"

Katie was gazing fiercely at Georgia as if willing her to remain silent. Georgia met her eye, and then she turned and smiled at Olivia, saying very clearly, "I've got something to say. I should have spoken up before. Yesterday Katie told me that Olivia was in for a nasty surprise and then today I saw Katie coming down the stairs before the lesson began. Katie threatened to tell everyone about a lie I'd told if I said anything about it."

Katie's colour rose and her eyes flashed with fury. "Don't believe a word she says. She's a terrible fibber! She makes things up all the time," she shouted.

"Yes," said Georgia quietly, her voice breaking with emotion. "I did make something up. And I'm really ashamed. I said that my mum was rich and that we were going to New York for Christmas. But we're not. We're poor; I wouldn't be able to come back next term if Miss Swan hadn't given me a scholarship. It was a silly lie and I only said it to make myself feel better, but it just made me feel worse and it made me weak because Katie used the fact she knew it wasn't true to make me do what she wanted." Her voice choked. "So there, now you all know, I'm a liar and not to be trusted."

There was a tiny bubble of silence, then Aeysha stepped forward, taking Georgia's hand tightly. "Yes, now we know," she said, "and I for one don't care. I like you, Georgia, for who you are, not for how much money you have. And you really deserve to have a scholarship."

"You do, Georgie girl," said Tom. Others crowded around Georgia. Katie watched, standing all on her own, her face white with rage.

Chapter Thirty-Seven

Abbie and Sebastian Shaw knocked on Miss Swan's study door. Inside, Alicia put down her pen and sighed. It had been a long and mostly unpleasant day. Her nerves still hadn't recovered from seeing Olivia almost plunge to her death from the tightrope wire, and her attempts to contact Jack, who she felt should know what had happened, had proved fruitless. Not only that, but she was mortified to discover that so much had been going on in the school without her knowledge and that Olivia had found her so unapproachable she had kept her tightrope-walking a secret.

To top it all, there had been the disturbing scene in her study when bit by bit the story of Katie's behaviour had come out, including the revelation that she'd cheated in the maths test. At first Katie had blustered and denied everything, but she soon broke down and admitted having put the earrings in Olivia's case to frame her.

Alicia had sent Olivia away while she talked to Katie alone, but it soon became apparent that Katie wasn't really sorry for what she had done – just sorry that she had been found out.

"You realise that I have no choice but to ask you to leave the Swan?" said Alicia gently.

"That's not fair. My dad said if I came here I'd be a star," whispered Katie.

"The Swan doesn't need stars, it needs children who will work hard and work hard together," said Alicia sadly.

Not long after this, Katie's dad had arrived and Alicia had a long and difficult interview with him in which he first threatened to sue the school and then offered Alicia a bribe to keep his daughter there.

"I'm sure you could do with expanding your premises," he'd said smarmily. "I've had my eye on the building next door for some time. I expect I could snap it up cheaply. I could turn a neat profit by building luxury flats at the top and you could have the bottom floors for more rehearsal space. Maybe even a new theatre. You have to admit the old one is a bit shabby."

"That's part of its charm," said Alicia drily, declining the offer and showing father and daughter the door.

Mr Wilkes-Cox refused to leave quietly, shouting, "You'll regret this! Wait and see. Nobody treats my girl like this. She's going to be a big star, aren't you, Katie?"

There was a silence.

"Aren't you, Katie!" thundered Mr Wilkes-Cox.

"Yes, Dad," said Katie, her chin in the air, but her eyes glistened with tears.

Alicia felt sorry for Katie. No wonder the child was like she was with a father who thought money could buy you out of any sort of trouble. She sometimes wondered whether they ought to audition the parents as well as the children for places at the Swan.

She was sitting alone in her study thinking about Katie, and Olivia too, and how in very different ways she had failed them both, when she heard the knock.

"Come in," she said a little wearily. She looked up and smiled when she saw that it was Sebastian Shaw and Abbie, two of her favourite people. But their faces were serious and she wondered what bad news they could be bringing.

Chapter Thirty-Eight

"What can I do for you?" Alicia asked, her smile dropping.

Abbie spoke quickly. "We think you should come to the upper rehearsal room. There's something you ought to see."

"What is it?" asked Alicia, alarmed, convinced that some new catastrophe had taken place.

"It's nothing to be worried about," said Abbie, unable to keep her face serious any more.

"No indeed," said Sebastian, smiling. "In fact, it's rather astonishing. I haven't been quite as delighted since Toni's Juliet won her an Olivier award."

He held open the door for Alicia. As she passed up the stairs in front of them, he said quietly to Abbie, "I just hope she recognises this for the wonder it is. Alicia is a remarkable woman in many ways, but she does have her blind spots."

When Olivia had returned to the upper rehearsal room following her interview with Katie in the headmistress's office, she was only intending to grab her tightrope and leave. But she found Georgia waiting for her outside.

"Olivia," said Georgia. "I'm truly sorry. I'll quite understand if you despise me so much you never want to talk to me again. . ."

Olivia put up a hand to stop her. "Of course I don't despise you, Georgia. Anyway, it's over. Katie won't be able to hurt either of us again. Alicia has seen through her at last." She took Georgia's hand and squeezed it.

When she opened the door, she found Tom and most of the children from the class waiting for them. They broke into a cheer when she walked shyly into the room, and gathered round wanting to know what had happened. Olivia shook her head and said, "Katie is still with my grandmother. It looks bad for her."

"But the main thing is that you're entirely

in the clear?" asked Georgia. Olivia nodded.

"That's fantabulous," said Tom, "because you've got dozens of new pupils, Liv. They all think tightrope-walking rocks and they want to learn. I've told them that you are a complete slave driver, but they won't take no for an answer." He grinned. "I've also told them about our *Romeo and Juliet* scene and everyone is very keen to see it."

Olivia stared at him, shocked. "You mean, you actually want us to do it in front of an audience?"

"Don't look so worried, Liv. We don't have to keep it a secret any more. Let's enjoy it." Olivia looked uncertain, but the others all begged them to do it, and Abbie said quietly, "Please don't disappoint us, Olivia."

Eel jiggled about and declared loudly, "Honestly, Livy, you're being invited to show off by a bunch of people who leap at every chance to be in the spotlight even when it's only the fridge light coming on and who would never *ever* turn down an invitation to perform themselves. You should be chuffed to bits they want to watch you."

"I am," said Olivia, giving a little bow, and

her serious face broke into a smile that made everyone else smile too.

While Olivia and Tom were setting up, Abbie slipped away and came back with Sebastian Shaw, and the two stood at the back of the room open-mouthed as Olivia and Tom performed their high-wire act.

Chapter Thirty-Nine

Now Abbie, Sebastian and Alicia were seated in the rehearsal room waiting for the second performance of the day. Sebastian had rigged up a couple of lights, and William Todd, who was a brilliant pianist and composer, was improvising some background music. The lights went down and came up again and there in the spotlight on the high-wire were Olivia and Tom, acting out the moment during the Capulet masked ball when the two lovers meet for the first time.

Alicia leaned forward in her seat and a tiny meow of surprise escaped her lips as Olivia began to speak. Olivia didn't notice her grandmother's reaction. She noticed nothing except her Romeo moving towards her on the high-wire. Her brain knew it was just good old

Tom, but her heart and soul responded as if he was a boy she had only just met and fallen in love with. She danced along the rope and tumbled so the audience suddenly realised for the very first time what the phrase "head over heels in love" really meant.

The scene continued as Olivia moved lithely down the wire using her dexterity to mask Tom's lack of wire-walking experience in a way that made it seem as if his physical uncertainty was simply the awkwardness of first love. It felt exhilarating, as if their heads, hearts and bodies were totally synchronised.

This, thought Olivia to herself, *must have been what it was like for my mum and dad when they first met,* and she hoped one day when she was older she'd feel a love for someone with the same passion and intensity.

Her body curled around Tom's on the wire, their palms touched and it was as if there had been an exchange of electricity between them. Afterwards, in what became a Swan legend, some in the audience swore they'd actually seen a flash as their fingertips touched. To Olivia, it felt as though there had been. It felt as if both she and her Romeo were lit up from inside. They were completely, heart-breakingly luminous.

In a demonstration of perfect control, Olivia cartwheeled backwards along the wire until the two lovers were standing at opposite ends, separated from each other by a void made up of their parents' enmity. Suddenly, there was silence.

Olivia and Tom jumped down from the tightrope. Olivia felt completely drained and dazed, as if she'd run a marathon. She couldn't bear to look in the direction of her grandmother. But then there was a flash of green velvet. Alicia was on her feet. Tears were pouring down her face. She began clapping and calling "Bravo!" and everyone else clapped and screamed their approval, too.

Olivia took a step towards Alicia. Alicia took Olivia's hand and said, "You are a great actress like your mother, but you have one talent that she did not: you are a great tightrope-walker like your father. The combination is irresistible. Olivia, I was wrong about tightrope-walking. It's a skill and an art, and your father has taught you well. He must be a very great artist, and you will be, too."

* * *

Half an hour later, Olivia, Tom, Abbie and Sebastian were sitting excitedly in Alicia's study together and Eel was jumping around.

"It will work, I'm absolutely confident," said Alicia. "It honours Shakespeare's words but also intensifies them, as if distilling the very essence of first love itself. It was like watching joy, and it will make the audience feel joyful too if we frame it in just the right way. We'll get the rest of the cast to play the guests at the masked ball in a cross-discipline dance sequence, and we will put Olivia and Tom centre stage on the high-wire, a moment of stillness in the swirl of the dance followed by an explosion of love. We need to keep it very simple but with the right costumes, lighting and music, it will be very effective and completely original."

"But Olivia wasn't already in our team, so I'm not sure that we are allowed to use her," said Sebastian.

"I've checked the rules," said Abbie. "We won't be disqualified for doing it. You're allowed one substitution up until the finals, and now that Katie has gone, Olivia can take her place."

Everyone looked at Olivia.

"That is, if Olivia will do us the kindness of

taking part," said Alicia. "I don't want to force you, Olivia. It's a big favour to ask. Nobody will think less of you if you decide you don't want to do it. You haven't exactly had a good time here since you arrived."

"Of course, she'll do it," piped up Eel. "The honour of the Swan and the Marvell family is at stake."

"Well," said Olivia with a smile, "if you put it that way, how could I possibly refuse? Yes, I'll do it, but on one condition."

"What's that?" asked Alicia.

"That I can give up baby ballet and carry on high-wire walking with Tom."

"It's a deal," agreed Alicia.

"There's something else," said Olivia. "You've got to help us find Dad before he does something silly."

Chapter Forty

Olivia, Eel, Tom, Georgia and Aeysha sat with Abbie in a steamy café, eating iced buns. An old TV on the counter was tuned to a rolling news channel. Very soon they would have to set off for the Palladium, where the final of the Children's Royal Spectacular was being televised, to meet up with the rest of the cast who were going there straight from school. They had been to the costumiers to see the dress that Abbie was going to wear to play Liesl in *The Sound of Music.* It was a treat decreed by Miss Swan, who had said that as Olivia and Tom had been working non-stop over the last thirty-six hours, they deserved a break. They had been told that they could invite along a couple of others so Eel, Aeysha and Georgia had come, too.

"Oh, Abbie, your dress is *soooo* beautiful," sighed Georgia. "I wish I could wear a dress like that on stage."

"You will one day, Georgia, if you keep working really hard," replied Abbie. "In any case, maybe Miss Swan will put you up to play one of the children in *The Sound of Music*? They'll be holding auditions at the start of next term. Your singing has really come on beautifully. I'm sure you could do it."

"Could I?" said Georgia, looking both chuffed and worried at the same time.

"You could," replied Eel firmly, "but only if you believe in yourself."

"You mean a hundred per cent, like you believe in yourself, Eel?" teased Tom.

"Yes," said Eel, so seriously that everyone burst out laughing. "I'm the bestest."

"Best," said Olivia with a weary smile.

"Actually, she's got a point," said Abbie. "You do need a bit of self-belief in this business, because you get so many knocks along the way. I don't mean self-belief in a Katie Wilkes-Cox way, but in an understanding your real strengths and weaknesses way. I've been up for loads of roles that I haven't got and you just have to learn to live with it and realise that if you don't get the part, it's not necessarily because you're no good, but it's because you're just not what the director is looking for. It doesn't make you a failure."

Tom opened his mouth to reply, but at that moment Olivia stood up so suddenly that she knocked her lemonade over. She had gone quite pale and was pointing at the TV. The others turned to look. On the screen there were grainy pictures of Tower Bridge and large crowds pointing upwards, and the newscaster was saying that some kind of unauthorised stunt was taking place. A man appeared to be tightrope-walking across a wire stretched between the very pinnacle of the bridge's two towers!

All traffic on the road and down the river had been stopped and large crowds had gathered to watch. A camera zoomed upwards and captured the unmistakable image of the Great Marvello in its sights.

"Tower Bridge. It's just round the corner, isn't it?" said Olivia urgently.

"Yep, just a couple of minutes away," confirmed Abbie.

"You've got to show us the way!" exclaimed Olivia.

"We've no time," said Abbie, anxiously looking at her watch. "We've got to get to the Palladium." She saw Olivia's stricken face and the determined set of her mouth, and Abbie knew that Olivia would never be persuaded to leave for the Palladium until she had seen her father.

Chapter Forty-One

They ran through the streets towards Tower Bridge. As they drew closer, they could see the flashing blue lights of fire engines and police cars. They pushed their way through the crowds, who were all pointing upwards at the man on the wire. He was dressed like an old-fashioned silent-movie star with a bowler hat and a walking stick and he appeared to be holding a sack over his shoulder. He was doing a slapstick comedy routine, at one moment appearing astonished by his own prowess and at the next on the brink of falling off the wire.

The crowd gasped as he appeared to lose his balance, and then broke into fits of laughter as he did the splits and raised his bowler hat to them.

Olivia ran onwards, followed by the others. She passed a blonde TV reporter who was talking into a camera. "Experts believe that the stunt has been some time in the planning because of the intense preparation required and that the wire must have been put in place secretly last night—" The reporter broke off to listen to some information that was being fed to her through her earpiece.

"Breaking news," she continued. "The daredevil on the wire has been identified as Jack Marvell, otherwise known as the Great Marvello, who has pulled off similar feats in several capital cities across the world. He was thought to have retired from the limelight to run his own circus. Marvell is the widower of the great classical actress Toni Swan, who died tragically. . ."

The crowds were getting thicker, but Olivia threaded her way through towards the base of one of the towers until she was right at the front behind a police cordon. The others struggled in her wake but eventually caught up with her. Up above, Jack waddled along the wire, scratched his head as if puzzled, and started juggling with his stick and two balls he'd produced from his pocket. The crowd broke into gales of laughter.

"Look, Livy, he's doing fine. Are you satisfied now? There's nothing to worry about. Let's go or we won't get to the Palladium in time to go on," said Eel.

"All right," said Olivia reluctantly.

The others began to weave their way back through the crowd. As Olivia turned to join them, the crowd gasped and some people screamed. Olivia swung round again, just in time to see that Jack had momentarily lost his balance. But he just as quickly righted himself again. The crowd waited. He took a faltering step forward and stopped, a tiny solitary figure alone against the great desolate expanse of grey sky. Seconds passed and turned into minutes and still the figure didn't move. It was as if he had been frozen in mid-air.

Olivia moved forward, squashing herself up against the police cordon and one of the policemen put a restraining hand on her shoulder. Olivia looked desperately around. She had to get to her father and help him before he fell from the wire. The crowd were murmuring, wondering what was going on. Still the tiny figure didn't move. Abbie, Eel and the others had made their way back to Olivia, who was staring purposefully at the wall of policemen in front of her.

"I've got to get through," she said desperately to the policeman in front of her. "That's my dad up there." The policeman shook his head disbelievingly.

At that moment, the crowd gasped. Buffeted by the high winds, Jack had almost tumbled off. He took another tiny step and faltered again. Apprehension passed through the crowd. Olivia was terrified, convinced that Jack was having a breakdown on the wire as he had before. She had to help him before he became completely paralysed in mid-air, unable to move either forwards or backwards, and easy prey for the rising wind that would knock him off his perch. She refused to think about the dark swirling waters of the river below, with its terrifying current that could drag a man to his death in seconds.

"Create a diversion!" she whispered urgently to the others. Eel immediately let out a loud scream and fell to the ground. The rest of them looked at each other for a split second and then did the same. Their acting was so convincing that the policemen broke the cordon and moved towards them to see what was causing the disturbance.

Olivia immediately seized her chance. She broke forward, dodged two policemen who tried to catch her, and ran to the tower at such speed that she knocked straight into the policewoman guarding the door at its base, winding her badly. Olivia entered the tower, slammed the door shut behind her, realised that the key was still in the lock and quickly turned it.

From outside she heard somebody shout her name.

"Olivia! It's me, Pablo. Let me in." She ignored him. She climbed as fast as she could up the stairs. At the top she was met by another policeman, who tried to grab her but she kicked his shins so hard that he doubled over in pain. She squeezed through the window, looking for where Jack had fixed the wire so she could climb to the very pinnacle of the tower and on to the tightrope.

The policeman had recovered and was shouting for help as he grabbed her feet and pulled. But Olivia kicked out as hard as she could and he let go. In that moment she scrambled out on to the tower, clambered up the final couple of metres and stepped out on to the wire.

"Come back!" called the policeman, but it was too late; his words were blown away on the wind as Olivia took another step forward. She shivered. She had never been on a wire in such treacherous conditions; the wind seemed to be delighting in trying to whip her off. She took another careful step and looked up. At the other end of the wire, she saw her father's face, his eyes wide, his mouth gaping in astonishment and horror. He shook his head as if he couldn't believe what he was seeing. Then he shook his head again, as if forbidding her to come any closer.

The wind caught her and it felt as if someone had punched her very hard in the small of the back. She steadied herself and tried not to think about the immense drop beneath her and the dark waters below. She took another step forward, gaining confidence, and took several more. She was only ten metres or so from Jack. She took another step towards him, smiled and put out her arms. He broke into a smile and put out his arms. She waved and he waved back.

Then Jack began moving nimbly towards her as if he hadn't a care in the world.

Down below in the gathering darkness, the crowd erupted with excitement. They thought this must all be part of the act. One person on the tightrope had been thrilling enough but two meant double the excitement! They roared their approval. The TV journalist became hyperactive, throwing her arms around madly, and the TV cameras zoomed in as Olivia and Jack hugged in the middle of the wire.

"What on earth do you think you're doing?" he shouted.

"Trying to help you," Olivia yelled back.

"Well, as you're here, you'd better make yourself useful," her dad grinned. "Hold these," and he passed her the sack and the cane. Before she could stop him, he had flipped over and was standing on his hands. He tumbled his way along the wire and back in an exhilarating display of acrobatics. The crowd whooped and clapped. He pointed to the sack, and Olivia opened it and pulled out a unicycle.

As she handed it to him, he shouted, "You'll find an umbrella in there too. Once I'm mounted and away, open it up and give it a twirl." Olivia watched her father mount the unicycle and find his balance. He began to pedal. Down below, the crowd cheered and thousands of camera phones flashed. Olivia pulled out the umbrella, which was unexpectedly heavy. Taking care so it wasn't caught by the wind, she opened it. Showers of silver and gold confetti fell from the inside down on to the heads of the crowds below, who went crazy.

Jack dismounted from the unicycle, took his daughter's hand tightly in his own and they bowed together. The crowd screamed and shouted their approval.

Jack kissed Olivia's cheek. "I couldn't have done it without you, chick," he said.

Chapter Forty-Two

The Swan cast stood on the stage of the Palladium, looking tense. They were waiting for the results. The voting was over, the telephone lines had closed and in just a few minutes they would know whether or not they had made it through to perform in front of the Queen. There were five acts left in the competition, but only three would be on the final bill.

Please, please, let it be us, thought Georgia to herself. She knew that, somewhere out in the audience, her mother would be sitting watching and Georgia wanted to make her really proud.

Olivia looked down and smiled at Eel, who was jiggling with excitement beside her, and then looked nervously across to the wings where Miss Swan, Abbie and Sebastian were all waiting expectantly. Abbie grinned and raised both hands with her fingers crossed. Sebastian put his thumbs up. Olivia felt both exhausted and exhilarated.

They almost hadn't made it to the Palladium in time. When Jack and Olivia had descended from the tower, they had been met by several grim-faced policemen who seemed intent on arresting them, despite the fact that the crowd were cheering and going wild trying to get near enough to congratulate them. Even the TV reporter had become incoherent with excitement.

"How does it feel for the Great Marvello to be back?" she asked Jack flirtatiously.

"It feels great to be back where I belong," said Jack, "and it's all down to my daughter Liv, and her love and support."

"He is the greatest," said Pablo, who had appeared with several magazine photographers in tow and was busy trying to negotiate exclusive deals.

Abbie and the others fought their way over to them.

"Olivia, we've got to go!" said Abbie desperately. Olivia raised her arms helplessly. A more senior policeman pushed his way towards them.

"Where have you got to go?" asked Jack.

"To the Palladium – we're in the final to perform at the Children's Royal Spectacular."

"You too, Liv?" asked Jack wonderingly.

"She's the STAR," said Tom.

Jack looked thoughtfully at his daughter. "You're full of surprises, chick. Some of them nice and some of them nasty. I almost died when I saw you up there on the wire." He took her hand and squeezed it. "You shouldn't have done it. You could have been killed. But I'm glad you did. I'm very proud of you." He looked around at the cheering crowds and TV cameras. "They seem to have liked it."

"It was a triumph," said Pablo happily. "Your dad, Olivia, he is the best tightrope-walker in the world, and you are a chip off the old block."

"Right then," said the police inspector. "I need your full names and addresses."

"She hasn't got time to give you her name and address, she's got to come with us," said Eel.

"She won't be going anywhere for quite

some time," replied the inspector ominously.

"But it's a matter of life and death; we'll be disqualified if she doesn't come now!" said Eel impatiently.

"Disqualified from what?" asked the inspector.

"The finals of the Children's Royal Spectacular," explained Abbie. She looked at her watch. "It starts in just under an hour. If we don't go now we'll be disqualified."

"You're having me on," laughed the inspector, but then he looked at Eel, Georgia and Aeysha and a flash of recognition crossed his face.

"I know you, I saw you on TV in the last round. You're from the Swan, aren't you? You were fantastic. We voted for you, the wife and kids and me. We all want you to win."

He looked at Olivia as if trying to make up his mind and then he said, "Strictly speaking, I'm not sure you've broken any law, apart from damaging the shins of one of my policemen. Go on, get on your way. We'll give you a police escort to get you to the Palladium. It's your dad I really need to speak to anyway. Good luck."

Which was how they had arrived at the

Palladium in two police cars with their sirens wailing and just ten minutes to spare. They were met by Alicia and Sebastian, who had hurried them into their costumes and on to the stage.

Olivia didn't even have a second to feel nervous. She just remembered standing on the wire and seeing Georgia giving her an encouraging smile. Then she was entirely swept up by the performance. She was Juliet. She was fourteen and living in Verona. She was experiencing all the excitement of her very first ball. She saw her Romeo and it was love at first sight. She was head over heels. Her life would never be the same. Her heart soared. Time stood still. Her fate was sealed.

The judges had looked sceptical when they had spotted the tightrope, but by the end they were on their feet with everyone else, declaring the performance the unexpected triumph of the series.

"It doesn't guarantee that the public will like it. They can be fickle," warned Alicia, but she couldn't stop smiling.

Now the moment of truth had arrived. Olivia stood on the stage between Tom and Georgia, who were both squeezing her hands so tightly it hurt. She grinned at Georgia, who grinned back at her. Georgia had spotted her mum in the audience, who had given her the biggest grin of all, to let her know Georgia had made her the proudest mum in the whole world.

"This is the moment you've all been waiting for," said the presenter. "The lines are closed, the votes have all been counted and I can tell you that the first of the three acts going through to perform at this year's Children's Royal Spectacular is. . ." He paused for dramatic effect. "The Treetops School of Dance and Drama!" The children leapt around and hugged each other.

"The second act through is . . . Pearl, the youth break-dance group from Manchester." There were more screams and cheers.

"And the final act through, topping the bill at the Palladium, is. . ." There was another long pause and then he said two words: "The Swan."

The stage and auditorium erupted, and in the mayhem Olivia looked across into the wings and saw that Jack was there. He was standing right next to Alicia, and they were hugging each other and crying.

* * *

Later that evening, Olivia, Eel and Jack were all sitting in Alicia's flat. They had just finished watching a recording of the televised show and were demolishing the final scraps of takeaway pizza. Jack's phone went off and he went into a bedroom to talk to Pablo. Eel had been on YouTube and announced that the clip of their performance had already had 200,000 hits, and the one of Olivia and Jack on the high-wire over Tower Bridge even more.

"Bet it will be up to half a million by tomorrow," she said with a satisfied smile. "We'll all be famous!"

"Stage-school brat," said Olivia, but her eyes were laughing. Jack came back into the room. He and Pablo had to report to the police station tomorrow, but the inspector had made it clear that charges were unlikely to be brought.

"Actually, they ought to give you a medal for cheering up London," he had said.

Offers of work had also been flooding in since the stunt, with one big North American circus asking Jack to name his price and a Las Vegas hotel offering him a residency with double the money if Olivia came too. Newspapers wanted exclusive interviews and a TV company wanted to fund his next stunt and make a documentary about it.

Jack smiled at Alicia and sat down on the sofa. Both Olivia and Eel snuggled up to him.

"Girls," he said seriously, "we need to talk about our future."

Eel looked at him anxiously and started wriggling around on the sofa with nerves. She opened her mouth to speak.

"Listen to what your father has to say," said Alicia, silencing her with a single look.

"I've had lots of offers," said Jack, "and there are some that are very tempting, although I'm not sure Las Vegas is really me. But I've had one offer that I'm minded to accept, but I want to run it past you two first, because if I do say yes then it will affect you both."

"What is it?" asked Olivia, her heart thumping.

Jack smiled at Alicia.

"Your grandmother intends to make circus training part of the curriculum from next term and she's invited me to become the Swan's Head of Circus. I love teaching and it would give us a steady income and somewhere to live. But," he paused, "it would also mean that you two could stay here at the Swan to continue your education and training."

Eel gave a whoop of joy and threw herself at Alicia.

"I knew it would make you happy, Eel," said Jack with a smile. "But what about you, Liv? I know you didn't want to come to the Swan in the first place, and your grandmother and I will quite understand if, after everything that's happened, you don't want to stay beyond the end of this term and the Children's Royal Spectacular performance over Christmas. Alicia has promised that Eel can stay on even if you decide against continuing, and we'll find somewhere else for you. Maybe you and I will even go back to Italy, and Eel can join us in the holidays. I promise to do whatever will make you happy, Liv. You don't have to say now. Please think about it."

"I don't need to think about it," said Olivia. "I *know* what will make me happy."

Everyone looked at her expectantly. Olivia took a deep breath.

"I never thought I'd hear myself saying this, but the Swan feels like home. It's where I belong, and what would make me happy is being here with Eel and with Gran. And being with friends like Tom and Georgia and Aeysha and Abbie. I've never really had friends before because we never stopped anywhere long enough to make them. I want to stay on at the Swan next term."

"Well, that's all settled then," said Eel happily, throwing herself into a mighty jiggle.

"Actually," said Olivia, "I don't think it is." Everyone looked at her, surprised. Her face was serious. She turned to Jack.

"I know you're a great teacher, Dad. You're the best. But do you really want to be one? Term in, term out. You have a circus soul, Dad, just like Eel has a dancing soul and Mum had an acting soul. You'd get restless here, and after a while you'd feel as if we'd tied you down. You'd be like a caged bird always dreaming of flying away. I couldn't bear that to happen to you."

"But we could all be together here," said Alicia. "Surely you're not proposing that your father abandons you again and sets out on another of his wild adventures." There was an edge in her voice.

"That's exactly what I *am* proposing," said Olivia quietly. "But Dad isn't abandoning us, we're setting him free. He'd shrivel and die here at the Swan; he needs to be constantly on the wing. Like that spirit, Ariel, in *The Tempest*. I've been reading it."

Jack was looking at his elder daughter and his whole face was suffused with love. "My Liv, chick," he whispered.

"It would be totally irresponsible behaviour," huffed Alicia.

"No, it wouldn't," said Eel, hugging Olivia and Jack. "It's the rightest thing to do in the whole world." Olivia looked at Jack and he gave an imperceptible nod, and all the tension went out of his face. He looked like a boy again.

"You're right, Eel," said Olivia. "It *is* the rightest thing to do. But we'll only let him do it on one condition."

"What's that?" asked Jack worriedly.

"We want you to tell us everything you remember about Mum. How you met, when you fell in love, how you got married. And we want to see all the photos and mementoes in your box."

"It's a deal," said Jack, his voice tight with emotion. "But you will join me in the holidays, won't you? I couldn't bear not to see you."

They nodded.

"And you'll be welcome here any time, Jack," said Alicia, and to her own surprise realised that she really meant it.

"A toast. We should have a toast," said Eel, raising her glass. The others raised theirs in turn.

"To Dad, may he have many adventures," said Olivia, her glass of lemonade held high. She caught Alicia's eye. "And to the best school in the world. Here's to next term at the Swan. Whatever it may bring!"

To find out about further titles in the

Olivia

series and other upcoming Nosy Crow books visit

www.nosycrow.com

To read an extract from

Olivia Flies High

turn the page!

Chapter One

Olivia Marvell jumped lightly on to the low wall outside the stage door of the Duke's theatre, flipped forwards on to her hands, and walked the entire length of the wall upside down as if it was the most natural thing to do in the world. Her little sister, Eel, and her friend Aeysha clapped enthusiastically. Several passers-by walking down the passage that divided the Duke's from the New Vic theatre next door stopped to applaud too.

Olivia flashed them a shy grin as she jumped gracefully down, wiped her hands on her jeans and said impatiently, "How much longer? They've been yonks. I'm going to explode into a billion pieces if I can't tell them our news soon!"

A gaggle of children emerged from the stage door, adults in tow. Like all the children who had dribbled out in small groups over the last hour, they didn't look too happy. One of the girls was snivelling, and her mother, a glamorous blonde with sharp features, said loudly, "Silly man. That director wouldn't know real talent if it bit him on the nose. Never mind, Kelly, we've got bigger fish to fry. You're on the shortlist for that car commercial. It's much better paid."

"But I wanted to be in *The Sound of Music* and sing 'Do-Re-Mi'. . ." whined Kelly, her voice drifting into the distance as they walked down the passageway.

"Not long now; they're down to the last few," said Bert, the stage door keeper. He'd slipped out from behind his counter just inside the stage door to join Olivia, Eel and Aeysha. Nobody, not even Gus the theatre cat, got into or out of the Duke's without passing by eagle-eyed Bert. He prided himself on knowing everything that was going on and was a fount of delicious gossip.

"So do you think that Tom and Georgia will be cast in *The Sound of Music*?" asked Eel, doing the little wriggle that had given her her nickname.

Bert shrugged. "The longer they're kept back, the better it looks for them. But there's another group of kids coming back for a final audition this afternoon, so nothing's certain. The director, Jon James, and the casting director may not finally make up their minds for days. And of course Chuck Daniels'll be trying to stick his oar in."

"Who's Chuck Daniels?" asked Aeysha.

"He's important; he's the producer. He raised the money to stage the show. Anyway, they'll want to decide which kids they think will work well together in which teams. I doubt anyone will be told today, although I have known it happen."

"Teams? It makes it sound as if they're going to play netball," said Eel, wrinkling her nose.

"No," explained Bert with a smile. "There are six Von Trapp children without counting Liesl, but they'll cast eighteen children in the roles and split the children into three teams. Each team rehearses and performs together and the three teams share the eight performances a week between them. That way nobody gets too tired. But it does mean auditioning a lot of children."

"I'd hate to have to do an audition," said Olivia vehemently, pushing back her curtain of dark hair. "If I had to choose between going to an audition and going to the dentist for a filling, I'd choose the dentist."

"You're just weird, Livy," said Eel, pirouetting very fast across the passageway and causing a man in a pinstripe suit to glare at her. She came to a stop with her chestnut curls still dancing and said, "Oh, I wish, I really, *really* wish that I was auditioning," so dramatically that Olivia, Aeysha and Bert smiled at her heartfelt passion.